WPK
9/11

Traitor's Kiss

Traitor's Kiss

Pauline Francis

USBORNE

First published in the UK in 2011 by Usborne Publishing Ltd., Usborne House, 83-85 Saffron Hill, London EC1N 8RT, England. www.usborne.com

Cover photography: PhotoAlto / Alamy

A CIP catalogue record for this book is available from the British Library.

JFMAM JASOND/11 00510/1

ISBN 9781409527411
Printed in Reading, Berkshire, UK.

"I know I have the body of a weak and feeble woman, but I have the heart and stomach of a king."

Queen Elizabeth I, 1588

✿ The Tudor family tree

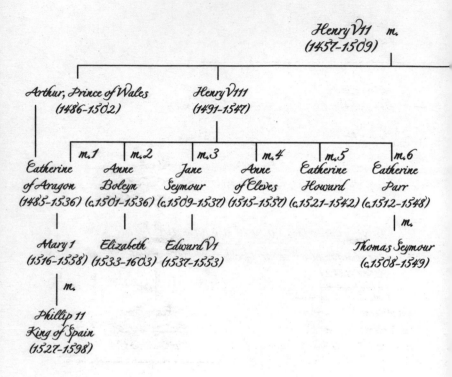

Henry VII m.
(1457-1509)

Arthur, Prince of Wales
(1486-1502)

Henry VIII
(1491-1547)

| | m.1 | m.2 | m.3 | m.4 | m.5 | m.6 |

Catherine
of Aragon
(1485-1536)

Anne
Boleyn
(c.1501-1536)

Jane
Seymour
(c.1509-1537)

Anne
of Cleves
(1515-1557)

Catherine
Howard
(c.1521-1542)

Catherine
Parr
(c.1512-1548)

m.

Thomas Seymour
(c.1508-1549)

Mary 1
(1516-1558)

Elizabeth
(1533-1603)

Edward VI
(1537-1553)

m.

Phillip 11
King of Spain
(1527-1598)

m. – married

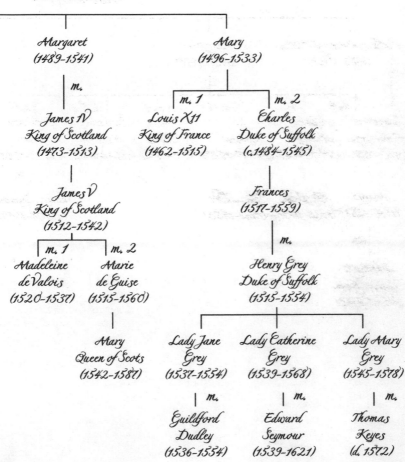

Elizabeth of York
(1466–1503)

Margaret
(1489–1541)

Mary
(1496–1533)

m.

James IV
King of Scotland
(1473–1513)

m. 1

Louis X11
King of France
(1462–1515)

m. 2

Charles
Duke of Suffolk
(c.1484–1545)

James V
King of Scotland
(1512–1542)

Frances
(1517–1559)

m. 1

Madeleine
de Valois
(1520–1537)

m. 2

Marie
de Guise
(1515–1560)

m.

Henry Grey
Duke of Suffolk
(1515–1554)

Mary
Queen of Scots
(1542–1587)

Lady Jane
Grey
(1537–1554)

Lady Catherine
Grey
(1539–1568)

Lady Mary
Grey
(1545–1578)

m.

Guildford
Dudley
(1536–1554)

m.

Edward
Seymour
(1539–1621)

m.

Thomas
Keyes
(d. 1572)

Prologue

Hatfield Palace, Hertfordshire
21 January, 1549

A scream comes through the open window, so piercing that it stabs me into waking. Who is it?

Kat will know.

But Kat is not in her bed, although her clothes are scattered on the floor, twisted like bodies in the gathering light.

I run downstairs, two steps at a time. At this hour, laundry maids should be crossing the courtyard. Master Parry should be giving orders to the servants. Roger

Ascham, my tutor, should be in the schoolroom, for he likes to read before breakfast.

But all is silent, except for the distant thud of horses' hooves and the wind whining between the tall chimneys.

Something is wrong.

"KAT! KAT!" I stand under the oak and scream into the wind. Dawn lifts the mist around its crown and softens the frozen grass that chills my bare feet.

I am Princess Elizabeth, daughter of King Henry the Eighth and Anne Boleyn, both dead. Kat is my only constant now. Without her, I do not know what to do.

Shall I pray? No, I do not want to kneel. When my mother knelt for her execution, she did not know that the sword was already hidden under a heap of straw; so the swordsman struck off her head suddenly, from behind, and she knew nothing of it. Full of pity for her, he had taken off his shoes so that she would not hear him coming.

That is the only good thing I have ever heard about my mother: that she died swiftly. As for how she lived, I have had only gossip to tell me.

"KAT! Where are you?" The wind hurls sleet into my mouth.

"Call as much as you want, but she will not come." It is a man's voice, just behind me. His peppermint breath warms my neck. He must have crept from the shadows of the tree with the stealth of my mother's swordsman. I turn my head, take in his short hair and beard, his face bloated from Christmastide although Twelfth Night is two weeks past. Envy bites. I was not at court. The new King – my little brother Edward – did not invite me.

I recognize this man. He was a gentleman in my father's privy chamber and Master of the Horse to my stepmother, Catherine Parr, when she was Queen.

I shift from one frozen foot to the other. "Sir Robert Tyrwhitt?" His bow is so brief that he hardly bends his back. "What brings you uninvited to my draughty palace on a winter's day?" I try to keep my voice light, like the snowflakes settling on our heads, but I am chilled with fear. "Where is Kat?"

"Mistress Ashley? She has gone away for a while."

His voice slaps me like the wind.

That is what they said when my mother stopped

coming to see me. I am two years old again and my throat tightens at the memory. I burst into tears as I did then, although I dislike the taste of salt. Now I tug at the collar of his fur cloak. "Is Kat dead?" I ask.

"She might be soon," he whispers. "She has gone to the Tower with your steward. He was the one who screamed just now."

"Why?" My voice dies in my throat.

He stares straight into my eyes. "To find out the truth," he says.

It has come to this. In my heart, I knew that it would. Too many things happened last year when I went to live in London. But Kat has done nothing – except love me. My tears double. I know what truth-seekers are like. I am one myself, and it has taken me to a place worse than hell.

With little concern for my tears, Tyrwhitt commands me to meet him in the schoolroom when I am dressed.

I stiffen. I am a princess. *I* give the commands.

It is my palace. Not his.

Then he is gone, in a swirl of snowflakes, as if I have dreamed him, and I stumble back to my bedchamber, drenched with sleet, reeking of fear – and anger.

Why did I blubber like a baby in front of Tyrwhitt? He will think I am easy prey.

Have I learned *nothing* this past year?

Kat has not laid out my clothes. Blanche Parry has not brought water for me to wash. I call for her; but she does not come either. I run backwards and forwards, like a headless hen, searching for something to wear. Where is the sombre silk from yesterday? Where are my velvet shoes?

I find the dress folded on Kat's chair. It stinks. But so do I now. I put it on, fastening the buttons wrongly so that the collar lies crooked and the bodice is not tight enough to stop my heart racing. I splash myself with Kat's perfume to hide my sweating fear and let my hair remain as crinkled as autumn leaves for I cannot find my comb.

There are wooden steps that lead from the garden to the schoolroom, and I take them instead of the ones from

 *13*

the Great Hall, although I am chilled to the bone. I want to look through the window before I go in. If Tyrwhitt does not choose his words carefully, he will feel the lash of my tongue.

The schoolroom window glows with candlelight.

I stand on tiptoe.

Tyrwhitt is seated in my tutor Ascham's chair. He has put on all his finery: his sleeves are of scarlet silk to match the feather in his cap. His fingers are as slender as mine, flashing their rainbow rings: emeralds, rubies and sapphires.

In this schoolroom, I learned to read and write at Kat's knee. Here I read Virgil and Horace and Cicero. It is a room for royal children, its walls warmed by tapestries and cushions, softened by books and maps, perfumed by ink and parchment and warm candle wax.

It is *my* sanctuary and I do not want Tyrwhitt in it.

He has seen me and opens the door. I go in, and in spite of my dishevelled appearance, he sweeps off his feathered cap in a deep bow. Then he waves me to my chair. Ascham always keeps his chair close to the fire.

Mine is close to the window and the garden door, for I hate to be shut in.

I remain standing, stamping my foot, forgetting that my brother, the King, must have sent him. "You cannot come to my palace unannounced and take my personal servants to the Tower without my permission," I protest, breathless.

"Oh but I can, Your Grace. The King's Privy Council has commanded it."

"Well, I am the King's sister and he will help me. And if *he* doesn't, I shall ask my stepfather, Thomas Seymour. He is the King's uncle."

"Your *stepfather*..." He lingers on the word, "...is no longer at home. He has also gone to the Tower."

I am slow to understand. "Is my *stepfather* to question *my* servants? He should have asked me first."

"Ah – no. He is a prisoner too."

My knees buckle.

Tyrwhitt waits for me to ask what he has done wrong. I do not. When I was very young – after my mother died – I learned one thing: if you watch in silence, you will hear more. I sink into my chair.

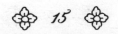

His chains of office clink as he fidgets. "Your stepfather, Thomas Seymour, has entered the King's bedchamber in the middle of the night, and killed his spaniel when it barked," he says. "He has boasted of becoming your brother's Protector...and of marrying you, now that his wife, Lady Catherine, is dead."

I want to cry again at the mention of Lady Catherine. She was my father's sixth and last wife. A few months after his death at Greenwich Palace almost two years ago, she married Thomas Seymour. I loved her dearly and I curse him in my mind. *He* is the reason that I did not see her before she died in childbed.

Tyrwhitt smiles like a fond father. "Let us talk of Thomas Seymour and you."

"There is no 'Thomas Seymour and me'. He is old enough to be... He is almost forty."

"Yet there are things" – he lowers his voice – "which you might want to confess to me now, before Mistress Ashley is forced to confess them...shameful things that we might attribute to, let us say, youthful folly."

The day has barely lightened beyond grey at the window. It was at such times that Thomas Seymour

came to my bedchamber… I am close to fainting. Hunger gnaws at my stomach. I have not eaten this morning. "What do you mean?" I whisper.

"You were seen in Lord Seymour's barge on the Thames last Shrovetide…alone…and before that…" He coughs.

The door creaks. Blanche Parry comes in, her eyes swollen with weeping. She does not look at me, but, clumsy with nerves, bangs a silver dish onto the table between us – a dish of sugar roses.

My breathing quickens. My cheeks flush. Nobody makes sugar roses for me here. I do not permit it.

Tyrwhitt *knows*.

I do not know how this will end, but I know how it began – little more than a year ago, when the leaves curled like flames, on the morning of my fourteenth birthday…

…with a sugar rose….

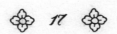

Chapter One

Chelsea Palace, London
1547

The door of my bedchamber creaked open, although it was not fully light outside, bringing in the sweet fragrance of sugar. I wriggled, mouth moist with anticipation, for Kat had promised me a birthday treat.

Fourteen years ago, on this day – the seventh day of September – my father had roared: "I gave up the Pope for *this*!"

"*This*" was me – another useless daughter like Mary, the daughter of my father's first wife, Catherine of Aragon.

The pain his words caused my mother must have been worse than the pains of childbirth.

My birthday. The day when everything was cancelled – beer, banquets and fireworks – because I was not the prince that would have saved my mother, Anne Boleyn. It was the day that marked her descent into despair. Her agony did not end with my birth, but continued for almost three years, until the last sharp pain of the sword.

I pushed these dark thoughts aside. Sugar! My teeth were rotting with it. But another scent came with the sugar, the sour and stale smell of the person who was carrying it. I got ready to scold the maid who had dared to bring her stench into my bedchamber, for, like my father, my sense of smell is keener than a bloodhound's. My pretty palace at Hatfield contains mostly fragrant women, and my male servants must suck peppermint pastilles if they come into my presence.

But I wanted Kat to have her surprise first. I closed my eyes and waited. Somebody lifted my hair and I thought it must be Kat herself. Something brushed against the nape of my neck, something rough and

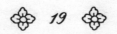

stinking of stale food. Confused, I twisted away from it, opened my eyes to curse whoever it was.

It was my stepfather, Thomas Seymour, bare-chested and bare-legged, carrying a cloth-covered silver dish. He stroked his beard, laughing at his own silly trick.

Part of me froze with fear. No man had ever entered my bedchamber, not even my father. No man had ever brushed my neck with his beard. And if Kat had to call a physician for me, she never left my side.

Disappointment slowly replaced the fear. Since my father's death in January, my stepmother, Catherine Parr, had invited me to leave Hatfield Palace to live with her and her new husband, Thomas Seymour. These last months had been the happiest of my life, in spite of my father's death, for I had grown to love my stepmother deeply. As for my stepfather, he was vain and arrogant, but he had always made me laugh, until now.

I did not know what to do.

My stepfather thrust the dish under my nose.

I backed away. "You frightened me, sir," I said. "What are you doing in my bedchamber? Where is Kat?"

He showed no shame. "Can a father not bring his

daughter a treat on her birthday?" he asked. "I wish you well today, Bess." I winced at his use of my pet name. He placed the dish on the bedcover between us and removed the cloth. In it lay a single sugar rose. It was white, although grubby at the petals' edges, and the cook had tried to disguise its greyness with gold leaf. "A perfect rose for a perfect rose," he whispered. "It was difficult for Maggie to make, Bess."

"My name is Elizabeth, sir."

"The rose is a secret flower, for its centre is hidden beneath so many petals…"

My skin tingled. My heart was beating too fast. *He* should not have brought it to me. *He* should not have brushed his beard against me.

"Eat it now," he went on. "Maggie says that she has put too much water on the petals and they may not hold together for long."

I kicked him in fury. He laughed softly and caught hold of my feet, tickling my toes. My spine tingled. Then he took my hand and ran his fingers up my arm. To my confusion and disgust, I did not want him to stop. I *wanted* him to tickle my neck again.

Then he forced open my clenched hand and placed the rose in my palm.

Disgusted with him, disgusted with myself, I threw it back at him. It split against his nose, showering sugar crystals onto his beard.

It is not in my nature to run, but run I did, as if the devil himself was after me: following the scent of sugar to the kitchen, through the back entrance into the garden, through lavender and thyme, until I reached a rose walk. Here I slowed to catch my breath. Some roses had been battered by last night's storm and their damp petals clung to the soles of my bare feet. Their heavy fragrance made my head spin and I glimpsed a shadowy figure reaching out to me; I did not know if it was friend or foe – or my stepfather.

I shuddered. "Who's there?" I whispered.

The air moved in the early shadows. Not as a dress or underskirt rustles. This was like the movement of a whole person, displacing the air around my head like the swish of a sword. I touched my neck, calling out wildly, "Show yourself!"

At once, the air stilled.

It was a sudden autumn gust, I told myself – or nothing at all. But how can nothing make the blood rush to the head, the spine shiver?

Chapter Two

Still afraid, I ran on…too far, for the gardens led down to the River Thames. It was the only thing I did not like about Chelsea Palace. I hated the stench of the river, for every privy in London empties into it. It was the only time I missed my sweet-smelling palace of Hatfield, where I had lived since I was a baby.

The stink of human filth brought downstream would have turned my stomach alone, but mixed with the Thames mud, it almost made me retch. That mud smelled of everything rotten: rotting meat, rotting vegetables, rotting fruit, rotting rats and cats...*everything* rotten.

Today, there was something worse than the stench. Silver eyes stared at me from the riverbank, dead eyes of dead fish abandoned in the mud by a high tide.

Women and children fought for every fish. Men, digging deeper with their hands, tugged out live eels. Some, forgetting their bellies, had gone for richer pickings: a rusted lantern, splintered wooden planks, a silk-tasselled cushion. Above them, fighting for the same spoils, gulls shrieked and swooped.

A boy was watching from an old rowing boat. When he saw me on the water steps, he jumped out and made his way towards me. I ran back up the steps, retching and breathless, but the smell followed me, so dank and fetid that I did not want to breathe at all.

I stopped and turned to face him. He was tall and straight-limbed, unlike the scavengers, whose legs and backs were bowed. His sturdy legs glistened with mud. Only weeping sores marred his handsome face. They flushed his forehead and cheeks, fading into his faint beard.

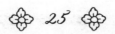

I had a strange feeling that I already knew him.

His clothes did not seem like the ones English men wore, but like those of the French men I had seen at court, though his lace collar was frayed, his breeches faded. And no man I ever knew of, whether English or French, would wear a woollen hat pulled over his ears.

"I won't harm you," he said. His voice was gentle – and a gentleman's, although it seemed from his accent that he was used to speaking French.

I paused, curious that he had not bowed or doffed his hat. "Do you know who I am?" I asked.

He took in my tangled hair, my night robe and my muddy feet. His small mouth broke into a surprisingly wide smile. "Yes," he said.

"Then you will know that I do not speak to men, except kings, princes, earls, dukes and lords – and *never* to strangers."

"My name is Francis, named for the great King of France."

"There is…was…only one great King – my father, Henry the Eighth."

"*I* was born in France."

 *26*

"And what is your family name?"

"I was born out of wedlock."

"So was I, so the Catholics say, although my father changed from the old faith to marry my mother, but—" I stopped. I was talking too much. "What do you want?" I asked. "If you have come to harm me, I am not afraid. I can kick and scream, and I have my own little dagger."

"My mother has sent me," he replied. "She…she made a promise to your mother…your *natural* mother, Anne Boleyn."

My heart tightened. After my mother's death, when I was two and a half years old, I had come to court only at my father's whim, or when his wives permitted it. It was forbidden to speak her name. I wanted Francis to say it again and again.

He saw the longing on my face. He understood it. For a moment, his eyes clouded like mine. "My mother, Alys, was your mother's lady-in-waiting," he went on. "Before your mother died, she made my mother promise…"

I put my hand to my neck, felt my racing pulse. "What…what did she promise?"

"…to tell you the truth about the charges against her. It was all your mother could bequeath to you. She knew what tittle-tattle you would hear."

They found twenty-one charges against my mother – all of adultery with five different men. A familiar fear tugged at my heart. How could I trust this boy? Had not my stepfather just tempted me with sweet things? Now Francis was tempting me with my mother. How I longed to hear the truth, but it was too much for my overwrought mind.

I raised my voice. "I have lived on lies all my life. It cost my father little to keep me when I was young, for I was fed on them." I glared at him. "Go away. I don't believe you."

Francis raised his hand. Something flashed silver.

So he is a French Catholic come to kill me, I thought.

I waited for the sword to take off my head. But he was stretching out his hand towards me. I saw that it was not the hand of a gentleman – he had toiled long and hard at the oars to earn such calluses. In his roughened palm nestled a silver box. As my eyes focused – I am short of sight – I saw my mother's falcon crest.

"Here's the proof," he said. "Your mother knew that you'd need it. My mother's kept it safe all these years. She says that she'll wait for you to seek her out."

"Why should I seek her out?"

"To talk about the truth," he said. "She'll wait as long as it takes."

My eyes blurred again – with tears. Every trace of my mother – crests, portraits, letters – had been burned, buried or banned as swiftly as her head had fallen into the straw. I had nothing of hers, except her swarthy skin and her piercing dark eyes.

I longed to hold the box. But I dared not take it.

"I know only too well of the gossip that comes from accepting gifts from strangers," I said. My voice choked with fear. "There is always a price to pay."

Yet I was holding out my hand as I spoke. Francis placed the box in my palm and its silver danced like lightning.

Years of fear overwhelmed me. Fear of gossip. Fear that I might be like my mother. I stamped my foot in the squelching mud. "How dare you approach me like a common pedlar who has fished a trinket from the river?

Tell your mother that I do not need it – or *her*." I hurled the box into the air and watched it gleam briefly before it sank into the stinking mud.

As soon as it had left my hand, I wanted it back.

I cursed my cruel words. I commanded Francis to bring it back. I commanded *him* to come back, but he was already dragging his boat into the water. And children were already searching for the silver box. I ran and elbowed them aside, digging until I had it in my hands. Astonished, the people around me laughed. Equally astonished at what I had done, I curtsied and laughed with them.

Only when I saw Francis rowing towards London did I realize the enormity of what I had done.

His mother might know the truth. But I had not even asked where she was.

I could not call Francis back. My stepfather was already waiting for me at the top of the steps, looking me up and down with derision. "I see that you have learned something new already, Bess. Mud sticks when it is thrown."

"I learned that before I came to the river, sir. Stay

away from my bedchamber," I said. "If it happens again, I'll tell Kat, or Lady Catherine."

"And who will they believe?" he asked.

Kat arrived having had difficulty keeping up with him, for she was small and her stride short. Her headdress was lopsided, revealing wisps of grey hair. Thomas Seymour turned on her, angry with guilt. "Mistress Ashley, why do you let the King's sister walk alone?"

She curtsied, scarlet with humiliation. "In Hertfordshire —" she began.

"This is *not* Hertfordshire, madam," he cut in. "Let her run wild there if you wish, but Chelsea Village is close enough to London to feel the evil shadows that walk its streets in search of innocence. It is your job to protect her and if you cannot, there are plenty who will." He turned to glance at the riverbank again. "Look at them," he said. "They're not human."

"I have come to no harm," I protested. "These people are not villains. They have little enough to live on. Let them take what they can. I might be Queen of England one day and it is the common people who will labour for me, fight for me and pray for me. Never forget them, my father used to say, and they will eat from the palm of your hand."

"And while you are feeding them, another will stab you in the back," Seymour said. He strode off without us.

Kat sighed. "Look at you – covered in mud. What will people think? You've made a fool of yourself – and me."

I did not care. I hugged the little box inside my night robe and my mother's crest calmed my racing heart.

A princess can never be alone. She is undressed, washed and dressed by maidservants. She can have no secrets. Kat called for hot water. Then she pulled my night robe over my head, catching my hair in the buttons, still smarting from Thomas Seymour's criticism.

The silver box tumbled with my clothes. As soon as Kat saw the falcon crest, she shrank back as if the devil himself squatted on the floor.

"Where did you get it?" she cried. "No…don't tell me. I don't want to know. Just get rid of it…or I'll do it for you…" She went to pick up the box, but I took it before she could.

"No, you can't have it!" I cried. I was two years old again and clinging to my favourite toy.

She washed my face and arms as if she would flay me alive. "You're too young to have seen people of the old faith buying holy water and scraps of cloth from Christ's shroud, and fingernails and teeth. Such relics have too much power." She drenched me with rosewater and wanted to use a strong perfume – the one the ladies at court wear. But I refused. Theirs was a heavy musky fragrance that made my eyes water. "That little box will bring trouble down on all our heads. Have you forgotten that everything to do with your mother is banned? Get rid of it, child, or one day…" She fastened me into my clean underskirt in silence.

My anger matched hers. "Don't you dare begrudge me this, Kat," I shouted. "You don't know what it's like to live without a mother, with only a succession of stepmothers to pity me or keep me from my father."

"You have Lady Catherine now. She doesn't pity you…" Her eyes flashed, jealous.

"…and she's the only one to ever treat me like a daughter and I love her. But this is my *mother*'s box." I clutched it close to me as she pulled on my dress. "Don't fret, Kat. That's all it is – a box. I'm not bringing my mother back from the dead."

"Aren't you?" she asked.

Chapter Three

"Where have you been, Bess?" Jane whined. "I've been waiting for hours." She wrinkled her little nose. "You *smell*," she said.

Lady Jane Grey is my cousin. She had been living at Chelsea Palace since the summer, until Thomas Seymour could arrange a good marriage for her, probably to my brother, the King. She was as small as a child of seven, although she was almost ten. I would have disregarded her when she arrived, but for the bruises on her arm.

It was well-known that her parents beat her. I pitied her, and she mistook my pity for kindness. She followed me everywhere, like a duckling follows its mother. Soon her hair was twisted like mine. Soon she wore pearls to flatter its golden-red. She walked like me. She talked like me.

Jealousy stabbed me as it always did when I saw her: because her nose was small; because she still had a mother; because she was clever, and because she was now a rival for Lady Catherine's affections and attentions.

I did not reply. I could not bear the sound of her chatter. That is why some people think that I am as changeable as the autumn wind. I *am*, but not by temperament. I have had to adapt myself to four stepmothers: Jane Seymour, Anne of Cleves, Catherine Howard and Lady Catherine. Only Lady Catherine has accepted me for what I am. Only with her was I truly beginning to be myself.

Jane waited no longer for a reply. "I was thinking while I was waiting for you, Bess," she went on. "Is it not strange that the three royal children are all motherless?" She giggled, nervous, because I did not reply. I was too angry. "But surely you'd rather have no mother at all than one who is a witch?"

"*What* did you say?"

"Mary said that your mother bewitched your father."

Mary is my half-sister, my father's first and only child from his marriage to Catherine of Aragon. She was brought up in the Catholic faith and still clings to it like a drowning sailor clings to a shipwreck.

"Oh, *did* she?" I said. "Of course, I forgot. Mary and your mother are close friends."

"They disagree about God so they don't talk about Him."

"So they slander my mother instead. Well, I've heard it all before, cousin. You can say nothing to upset me."

"Mary said that your mother poisoned hers. When the physicians cut open her poor dead body, they found black poison clutching her heart…"

I slapped her hard. Her thin cheek flared with the imprint of my fingers. "Take care, Jane. I'm the King's sister and second in succession to the throne. You're

only his cousin, so I'll be Queen of England before you if anything happens to him, or to Mary. And if I am... I'll..." I chopped the side of my hand across her thin neck.

She ducked away.

"STOP squabbling. I can hear you from the staircase." Lady Catherine had come into the parlour. Her voice was scolding but already full of forgiveness at our noisy behaviour, for these days she brimmed with love for Thomas Seymour, as she never had for my father. *"Ira furor brevis est."*

"Anger is..." Jane began.

"...a brief madness," I finished.

"Yes, remember that – it takes away reason," Lady Catherine said. "Jane, we do *not* gossip in this palace. Elizabeth, we do *not* use physical punishment in this palace." Then she laughed and made us kiss her. "I've always dreamed of such a family, for such squabbles are the stuff of life. They show there is strong affection."

As I kissed Lady Catherine's sweet-smelling cheek and murmured my apology, I suddenly ached for my own mother. "Why is everything different today?" I asked. "Why is everybody talking about my mother, when I have scarcely heard her name spoken these last years?"

She stroked my face. "Perhaps you notice it more because this is the day when *you* think of her more. But nothing can bring her back, Bess."

"I am fourteen years old, madam, and I still do not know what she did wrong. I used to let the maids pet me so that I could listen to their gossip. I wished I hadn't. If I were to believe them, her face was smothered with warts and moles and she had an extra nipple where the devil came to suck… But I did not expect to hear her cursed *here*, by my own cousin."

"I am sorry for what I said," Jane replied.

"And so am I," I said, ashamed. "I know that I have much to learn about people, for I have only lived with nurses and maids dedicated to keeping me in a state of happiness. Yet not one of them realized how unhappy I was."

"Let us pray to God that He can wipe out the bad memories for you," Lady Catherine said. "Jane, give Bess your gift."

 *39*

Jane handed me a small parcel wrapped in green velvet. I unfolded the cloth, which released a vile fragrance, like the smell of a fox or a cat. It came from a pair of dark green velvet gloves.

"Lady Catherine helped me to choose them," Jane said. "Perfumed gloves are the latest fashion in France."

"Think, Elizabeth," my stepmother said. "Perfume reminds us of people more than anything else. When you are an old lady like me, these gloves will remind you of the day we celebrated your birthday together. Put them on."

They fitted my elegant hands to perfection. And so I started my fifteenth year reeking like an animal.

My stepmother was wearing the brooch that my father had given her on their wedding day: three pearl teardrops gleamed against the bodice of her scarlet damask dress.

I asked, "Is your husband not jealous when you wear my father's brooch?"

"No. He insists that I wear it, especially when his brother, Edward, comes to dine, as he will tonight. Tom

wants everybody to remember that I was once the Queen of England. It makes him feel powerful. Tom is not a happy man these days, Bess, as you know. His brother has all the power as the young King's Protector, and he is jealous. This brooch says, 'Look! I have the former Queen of England as my wife, and the King's sister as my stepdaughter.'"

"So you are his trophy?"

"Yes, but I do not mind, Bess. I love him."

And I blushed with shame as I remembered my stepfather's beard brushing my neck. If he loved her as much as she loved him, he should not have come to my bedchamber.

Lady Catherine's gift to me was a book that she had written. It was called *Lamentation of a Sinner*. I inhaled the scent of its green leather and ink, fresh from the printing press, as I skimmed its pages. "*A wife must always obey her husband, whatever he chooses to do,*" I read aloud. "Must she obey him even if he chooses to murder her?" I asked.

"Your mother was tried according to the laws of our land," Lady Catherine said.

"Then the laws must be changed," I cried. I was on the brink of tears. "You were married to him, madam. Did he never speak about her? *Did* she bewitch my father and betray him?"

"I do not know, Bess. It was forbidden to mention her."

"If nobody will tell me, I know somebody who can," I cried.

I ran to my chamber, sat on the window seat and let the tears come. Then I took out the silver box from my writing desk and traced the falcon. I am an impatient person, yet I did not open it.

What if there was poison inside? I had been angry with Jane for repeating the gossip – that Mary thought my mother had poisoned Catherine of Aragon – but it was not the first time I had heard it. And my father's death had set Mary and me against each other. He had passed a law just before he died stating that Mary could only succeed Edward if she agreed to keep the new faith. If she did not, I would succeed in her place.

I pushed the evil thought away. Mary and I were still close, in spite of her hatred of my mother. She always said that I could not be blamed for her sins.

I was still crying when Kat came in. She glared at the box in my hand. "Bess, your father loved you and you loved him. Isn't that enough for you?"

"No, it isn't. You've been with me since I was four years old and you alone know that I was nine years old before I spoke to him in private. He couldn't bear to look at me all those years because I reminded him of *her*. Then suddenly he was taken with my wit and intelligence. As long as I didn't mention my mother, he was pleased to see me."

Kat put her arms around me and shed a few tears at my distress. "Oh, Bess, if only *I* had known her. I could have spared you this misery." I did not respond and she drew away. "Have I not been like a mother to you? Ah – you've got Lady Catherine now. You don't want me."

"I'll always want you, Kat."

She stroked my hair. "But your stepmother is right for once," she said. "You shouldn't let your mother haunt you from the grave. Let me take the box, Bess. Let me get rid of it."

I refused. Angry, she ripped a jet bead from the

bodice of her dress. "You may as well worship this," she said. "If you believe something has power, then it *will*. It's called superstition."

Kat threw the bead onto the floor. Then she went downstairs for breakfast. She could not persuade me to go with her. The thought of food sickened me. A man's beard brushing my neck, a stranger speaking about my mother... Who would not be disturbed by such events?

No, I did not dine that morning. Already I had too much to digest.

Chapter Four

Jealousy spread through the dining chamber that early evening like the autumn mists rising from the Thames.

Thomas Seymour's elder brother, Edward, had come to dine. When my father died, and my nine-year-old brother Edward became King of England, it was Edward Seymour who had proclaimed himself my brother's Protector. Thomas Seymour had never forgiven him for snatching the most powerful position at court.

 45

Edward Seymour and his wife, Anne, had brought Robert Dudley with them in their water barge. My heart leaped with pleasure at the sight of him. We were almost the same age and we had been friends since we were eight years old.

Since I last saw Robert, his thickening beard had been clipped short in the latest Italian fashion, although his moustache was still a faint shadow.

We were all out of sombre mourning clothes for the first time since my father's death seven months before. Robert's slender legs were clad in turquoise hose, in contrast to the orange silk that showed on his velvet sleeves and breeches. A short ruff stood clear of his silver earrings. An orange plume adorned his cap.

I stood by the window and let him come to me. He bowed and kissed my hand. "Hello, sweet Bess. I've missed you."

My arm tingled. I remembered how my stepfather had tickled my arm and I did not want to pull my hand away. "Hello, sweet Robert. Where have you been this summer?" The bodice of my new dress was so thick with pearls that I could not breathe deeply. Not for me the

fiery colours of the sun, but the colours of the moon: white and cream and silver – and pearls to cool my Tudor hair. I am not beautiful, I know that. My nose is too big for my face and my eyes are too small for it. My skin is sallow, like my mother's. But I am thought to be beautiful when I laugh and sparkle.

"My mother won't stay in London for fear of the plague." Robert was staring at me and I twirled around for him. "Am I beautiful?" I asked.

"You're like the moon and the stars," he said. "You're like the Queen of the Fairies."

"I don't believe in fairies."

"Neither did I, until I saw you," he replied.

How easily we slipped back into our childhood teasing. Robert handed me a sugar plate, wrapped in a silver cloth. Underneath were miniature marzipan oranges, each one bite-size, each one sparkling with sugar. I laughed. Jane clapped her hands, bright-eyed. I startled at the sight of her. I had not noticed that she was standing there.

"Robert and I used to steal oranges from my father's hothouse," I told her.

"Then we ate them hidden in the foliage," Robert said. He put a miniature orange into my mouth and one into Jane's. "Welcome to London, Lady Jane," he said. "Have you felt the lash of Bess's tongue yet?"

She blushed. Like me, she wore white. But white needs a woman's shape. It is not the colour for a puny body and pale eyes.

Thomas Seymour watched us. He repelled me, yet he made my heartbeat quicken. He filled the room with his presence, as my father had.

"Red Beard is scowling tonight," Robert said.

It was our nickname for my stepfather. Once I would have laughed. Now my eyes brimmed with tears, for I had felt so many emotions that day. "He's as cunning as a fox," I whispered. "He brushed my neck with that beard this morning and thought it amusing. Robert, he came into my bedchamber."

"What? You must tell Kat, or Lady Catherine."

I shook my head. "No. She deserves to be happy. I won't let it happen again."

"If he harms you, I'll kill him."

"Does he think I'm easy prey, Robert? Does he think

I'm like my mother?" Jane was listening, eyes widening. Dusk was casting its shadows across the garden and gusts of wind came in, bringing the stench of mud from the river. In my mind, I saw Francis's pale face, his livid sores, the silver box. "Go away, little cousin," I said. "We've grown-up things to talk about."

Robert gave her another orange and, reluctant, she left us.

I did not know how to begin. So I blurted it out. "Robert, will you do something for me?"

"Yes. Anything."

"Will you be my eyes?"

"If you'll be my lips." He leaned over, as if to kiss me. He had never done that before. We had played childish games together, but they had never included kissing. We were too well chaperoned. My heart quickened as it had when Thomas Seymour had tickled me. I *wanted* him to kiss me, but I drew away. Tittle-tattle had told me this was the sort of thing my mother had done.

"Ice Queen," he teased. "What will it take to melt you?"

"Be serious. I want you to find a boy for me…"

 *49*

He laughed. "Wouldn't you rather have a man? Who is he, this rival for my affections?"

"It's not *him*. I want to speak to his mother. She was my mother's lady-in-waiting."

"Ah... They're the most vicious. They're hard-hearted creatures, because they're close to power, but they don't have it. They're like ravens, pecking for scraps of gossip."

"My mother was one, don't forget, to Catherine of Aragon." I lowered my voice to a whisper. "Robert, she's promised to tell me the truth about my mother...whether she was guilty of those vile charges against her..."

He understood my need. He always has. But his eyes flashed with concern. "What can this woman tell you, Bess? There's always somebody who claims to know what really happened... Somebody who'll want something in return... And what if she tells you that your mother was guilty? What will you do? Search for somebody else to tell you otherwise?"

"I don't know. But I'll start with the boy. It won't be difficult to find him," I insisted. "He's a gentleman yet he doesn't look like one. He rows an old boat and wears a woollen hat."

"Then the whole thing stinks of skulduggery," Robert said.

"*He* stinks. You'll smell him before you see him." My heart was thudding. "He stinks of decay…and death."

"Then there's no use in asking me," Robert replied, "for I've no sense of smell."

"But *will* you do it – for me?"

"No, Bess." From the way he pressed his lips tight, I knew that he would not change his mind. "I'd do anything to protect you, but I can't, even if I wanted to. I'm only fourteen. I can't go anywhere alone either. My father…"

"Ah – your *father*," I scoffed. "John Dudley, the Earl of Northumberland, the man who craves power over the King as much as Thomas Seymour does. I thought you were a man. But you're still a boy."

"And I thought you a woman from today, Bess. But you're still a girl full of childish dreams." Already he was looking over my shoulder. He wanted fun and he knew that it would not come from me that night.

"I was never allowed childish dreams," I said. "Well, if you won't find him, then I shall."

❈ ❈ ❈

The table filled with food: swan, goose, capon, pigeon, partridge, pheasant. Anything that had once flown lay there. My father's wine glasses – a gift from Venice – had been brought out for the occasion and they gleamed. It was hard to remember that it was my birthday. So many strange things had happened. The happiness I had felt on seeing Robert had already drained away.

"Look, the cocks are preparing to fight," Robert said, trying to warm the coolness that had come between us. "Red Beard's loosening his ruff and his brother Blue Beard's loosening his cuffs. Now they're both stroking the feather in their caps." His smile faded. "It may be only brother against brother today, but I swear, Bess, that one day it will be Seymour against Dudley."

Thomas Seymour took the head of the table. Anne Seymour sat on his left, next to Robert Dudley and Lady Catherine. I took my place opposite Anne Seymour. Edward Seymour sat beside me, alongside Jane.

My stepfather raised his glass. "Let us drink to the good health of the Princess Elizabeth on her special day," he said.

❦ 52 ❦

"And to the new reign of Edward the Sixth," Edward Seymour responded. His deep-set eyes sparkled for the first time. He raised his glass. "To the King and all those who protect him. To my little brother Tom, now Admiral of the King's navy. May he protect us at sea as I protect us on land."

The brothers chinked glasses in front of me. "And to my brother, who takes what does not belong to him," my stepfather said.

We all stopped drinking. We all watched Thomas Seymour, who seemed to be staring at his sister-in-law's plump breasts. Indignant, she tried to pull up her bodice. But he was looking at her necklace, at the candlelight caught in every perfect emerald. I had not noticed them before. Now I stared too.

"I assume from your appalling behaviour, brother, that you have an axe to grind," Edward said.

"Unfortunate choice of words," Thomas replied. "But you are right. Your wife is wearing *my* wife's jewels and they hang ill on her old hen's neck. Such gems should lie flat so the light can catch the cuts. What is *she* doing with them?"

Anne Seymour defended the emeralds with her fleshy hands. Her neck, flushing now with anger, did the green no justice. "My husband gave them to me. In the absence of a queen, I am now the First Lady in the land."

I listened, enthralled.

"No, that honour belongs to *my* wife, the stepmother of the King of England," Thomas said.

Lady Catherine, alarmed, said firmly, "It doesn't matter, Tom. I don't like emeralds. They make my skin look sallow." She stood and raised her dress enough to show her shoes, encrusted from heel to toe with diamonds. "I prefer diamonds. They last for ever."

"Oh, but it does matter," her husband replied, his face grim. "They were given to you by the King of England and they should not have been taken from you."

Robert leaned across the table. "Peck...peck...peck. Who will take out the other's eyes first?" he whispered.

"Then let the King decide who shall have them," Edward Seymour protested.

"That poor little boy," Thomas sniggered. "He can't even empty his bowels without your say-so. No wonder they say that he is clogged with..." He gulped his wine.

"There is no more to be said. These jewels have belonged to every Queen of England for the last forty years, since Henry gave them first to Catherine of Aragon when they were married, and then to…" His voice trailed away.

"…and then he must have given them to my mother." I said the word lightly. It was strange to say it in public. "Emeralds are for constancy, and she was as constant to my father, the King, as the earth is to the sun." I laughed. It was my mother's laugh, halfway between despair and terror. Kat glared a warning.

The cocks stopped pecking. Blood glistened in their beards. Flesh flecked their teeth. Quietly, two of the most powerful men in England threw down their bones and licked their fingers.

The emeralds enthralled me. I could not look away. I got up and leaned across the table. I wanted to rip them from that ugly neck. But I did not do it. As they caught the candlelight, the precious gems must have caught a memory in my mind because I touched them gently, one by one. *I have only a little neck*, my mother had said on the scaffold. My heart ached for her.

Anne Seymour's neck pulse beat wildly. "*I* am fit to wear the Queen's jewels," she boasted. Her mouth puckered with disapproval as she glared at me. "*Your mother* was not. Your father feared her as much as we fear witches on All Hallows Eve. Her chamber was full of lotions and potions that she used to put a spell onto men. Five of them: Mark Smeaton…Henry N—"

"I know their names," I said. "Mark Smeaton. Henry Norris. William Brereton. Francis Weston. And George Boleyn, her brother. Tittle-tattle was my tutor, for nobody took the trouble to tell me the truth. Your vile words are not new to me, madam. They have followed me from the cradle and they will no doubt follow me to my grave."

"It is your misfortune that you grow more like her every time I see you," she said.

Her words finally released my pent-up anger. I leaned further across the table and tugged at the necklace. It snapped, showering the gems like hailstones on a stormy night. Some tinkled against the wine glasses. Others fell into the rush matting under our feet. Kat knelt to pick them up.

"Leave them," I said. "If she wants them, let her get down on her knees. That's what my mother had to do." I turned to Edward Seymour. "You were there, sir. Did they put down fresh straw for her head, or was it soaked with her brother's blood?"

"Your mother was England's most troublesome Queen," Edward Seymour replied. "She did not know how to hold her tongue, as you do not. Catherine of Aragon was a real Queen, the daughter of a King and Queen. She knew when to be silent. Tom, you're her stepfather – aren't you going to…?"

"Don't tell me what to do," Thomas Seymour spat. "You have the King, but I have the King's sister."

"*Nobody* has me," I protested.

"Bess," my stepmother pleaded. "Sit down. We are here to celebrate your birthday. You are not on trial."

"Oh, but I *am*," I said. "And as the daughter of Anne Boleyn, I am condemned by all of you."

I sat down. I did not know what else to do. Jane gaped at me. And under the table, Robert Dudley took my cold hands and squeezed warmth back into them.

✻ ✻ ✻

Kat scolded me for the second time that day as she combed my tangled hair late that night. "What's wrong with you, child?" she snapped. "You longed to come and live here when your father died. You love Lady Catherine, and now you're spoiling everything."

"I didn't know it would be so difficult. At Hatfield, there were few reminders of my mother. But it's different here. They see her in me, Kat. I didn't expect it." She tried to pet me, but I pushed her away, irritated. "You heard what Anne Seymour said. Once…just once, I want to hear somebody speak well of my mother." My words slurred. "Did she love me, Kat? How will I ever know?"

Kat did not reply. She had heard it too many times. She kissed me and blew out the candle.

Darkness is the time I think of my mother. When somebody – Kat was not with me then – told me that she had gone away – and not that she had died – I pretended that she was sailing the world to bring back treasure for me. I was only two when she left, so I could not remember her, except as a shadow. No face. No body. No voice.

 *58*

But tonight was different. Now I had something that my mother had held in her hand. In the moonlight, I saw well enough to fetch the silver box.

As it sat in the palm of my hand, that little box became as magical and as mysterious to me as the Holy Sacrament sitting on the altar. People of the old faith believed that the bread and wine became the body and blood of Christ during their Holy Mass. I did not. Yet part of me believed that my mother lay there, in my hand.

I touched the box briefly. For a moment, I was touching my mother. I sifted through my thoughts... through sights and smells and sounds...straining to remember her. But she was still that shadow – the shadow of a witch and an adulteress.

The first chime of midnight. Soon my birthday would be over. I eased the lid. The tiny hinges creaked. Then it flew open, releasing not all the evils of the world but a heavenly fragrance – the scent of roses and others that I did not recognize – that quickened my heartbeat, because I knew it.

It was my mother's perfume.

My maids at Hatfield Palace used to sprinkle

rosewater on the soft skin in the crook of their arm, on their wrists and behind their ears before they went to meet their sweethearts. I took some of the creamy perfume and did the same. Then I lay down and closed my eyes. I had seen them do that too, as if swooning at the memory of something beautiful.

In the warmth of my bed, the fragrance deepened, suffocating me, and I feared that it *was* poison. Then the shadows sharpened into a clear shape – my mother, not as a ghost, but as flesh and blood. I saw her with my child's eyes. I smelled the same fragrance on her skin.

My heart turned over.

I am two years old again. We are in the nursery at Hatfield Palace. I can see my little bed, with its silver-tasselled counterpane. I can see myself clutching the neck of a grey rocking horse, squealing as it lurches backwards and forwards. The green satin ribbons in my hair swing like the emeralds around her neck. My mother is holding me by the waist and every time I squeal, her lips pucker in a kiss to my cheek. Then her silk-soft hair brushes my cheeks like butterfly wings, and tickles my nose until I sneeze. I knew that her eyes

were dark, for mine are like hers, but now I know that they shone with love for me.

"Oh, what a perfect little rosebud you are," she whispers. "You will grow into the most beautiful rose England has ever known."

Slowly, on the last chime of midnight, her voice fades and with it her face, her fragrance, her body.

Now I understood. *Perfume reminds us of people more than anything else.* That is why I had felt the air rustle in the rose walk. It had been a half-memory, the fragrance not strong enough to bring her whole to me. My heart swelled with love for her. Yes, she left me. But she had left me her most precious gift – her perfume box.

As I drifted in and out of sleep, I hugged the first truth about my mother: she had looked at me with love.

Chapter Five

It must be like falling in love, I thought.

I have never been in love. But from what I have heard from the maids, the feelings that I had the next morning came close to it. I wanted to stay with my mother. I wanted to think about her all the time. I wanted to see her again and again. The faint fragrance on my skin still brought her to me. She was softness and light and silkiness.

But I could not stay in bed. I liked my little

bedchamber, with its soft bed and its window seat looking onto the Thames and the turning windmills on the opposite bank. There were birthday roses on the mantelpiece, releasing their fragrance in the firelight.

Until yesterday, I had felt safe. But now I would not risk my stepfather returning. I would walk in the garden early, although I would not go as far as the river.

I wrapped myself in my cloak.

Yesterday, I had run like the wind. Today, I ran downstairs on fairy feet, so light that I did not wake the caged parrots hanging in the corridor that led to the back entrance.

Outside the kitchen door, I paused.

I smelled sugar.

Once, when I was six or seven, I had wandered into my father's kitchens at Whitehall Palace. I had never forgotten the sight. His vast kitchens swarmed with young boys – not much older than me – in a heat so searing that they had taken off their clothes. The stench of their sweating bodies made me sick. Kat found me crying by the roasting spit. But it was not being lost that made me cry. In truth, with its writhing limbs and fire and roasting flesh, I thought I had entered hell that day.

Now the sweetness tempted me. I opened the door and went in.

This kitchen was my father's in miniature. Its low beams were hung with herbs – comfrey, camomile, feverfew, lavender and rosemary. Baking bread gave off its own sweet smell. The window sills were crammed with trays of sugared rose petals, ready to crisp in the first sun.

"Close the door, you fool," a voice called, so sharp that it could have taken off my head in a single blow. It came from a small room beyond the kitchen and I made my way there. It was a cool room with no windows, other than a small skylight in the roof. In the dim light, I could only make out three white shapes: a sugar loaf, a mound of paste and a face. As my eyes grew used to the darkness, I saw three women at work: breaking off sugar crystals; rolling out paste; cutting with a knife. It was the woman nearest to me who had the palest face. Above her top lip lay a cloth as ghastly as her cheeks.

My lips twitched at this astonishing sight. I laughed.

When the woman heard me, she gasped and sank into a deep curtsy, straining her once white apron across her plump body.

"Are you Maggie?" I asked.

She nodded, mumbling incoherent words. The kitchen maids giggled. Then Maggie laughed with us and her cheeks crinkled like an old vase. One of the girls ripped the cloth from Maggie's lip and it was streaked with black hairs, like flies caught in cream.

"Welcome, My Lady, Princess Elizabeth. I'm Margaret Payne, cook and confectioner." She winced as she spoke. "And these are two of my kitchen maids, Mary and Bess, named for you and your sister. Lord Seymour's brought us from his house in Gloucestershire, for he can't live without my sugared plums."

"Otherwise, he'd have to make do with stewed plums," Mary said. She giggled again, although I did not know why.

"What is wrong with your face, Maggie?" I asked.

"It's egg whites, Your Grace," she replied. "They lighten the skin better than morning dew. And there's nothing better than sugar paste for smoothing the upper lip."

Only then did I notice her swarthy skin, and dark hairs sprouting from her chin.

"I forgot, thank you for the sugar rose."

She blushed. "I hear that it weren't to your liking. Lord Seymour says I must try harder this morning."

"I don't want you to make any more," I said. My face flushed. "They are rotting my teeth."

Her face set, as if her egg mask had dried hard. "I take my orders from Lord Seymour," she said. "That's what he wants, so that's what he'll get."

She picked up a small kitchen knife and began to cut out the rose petals from the sugar paste. She curled their edges with the tip of a spoon. She stuck them together with water, one on top of the other.

Thomas Seymour was a clever man. He knew how much I craved sugar. But I would not let him deprive me of it. I reached across Maggie, snatched up the rose and crammed it into my mouth. Then I went to walk in the garden, leaving Maggie astonished and her maids giggling again.

My stepfather caught up with me under the roses. He sniffed as he bowed and kissed my hand. "Your perfume reminds me of the good old days when your father could joust and hunt and ride *and* rule England with an iron fist," he said. "When he was married to your mother…"

Yes, as cunning as a fox, and with a beard as bushy as a fox's tail. He would have enticed me with more titbits; but I pushed him away and went inside, calling for Kat to come and dress me.

I would not tell her yet. Lady Catherine loved him. And even if I swore Kat to secrecy, I could not trust her. Her tongue always loosened after wine.

A strange stupor slowed me over the following weeks.

Lessons that had once stimulated me dragged as I waited for the days to end. Master Grindal, my tutor, did not scold me. "Young girls need to daydream," he said.

As soon as darkness came and Kat had blown out the candle, I had what I wanted most: my mother. I craved her perfume like a man craves wine before sleep.

Every night, I opened the perfume box. Every night,

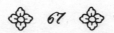

I permitted myself just enough cream on my skin to remember my mother again. With my child's eyes, I saw my mother in so many ways now... She wears scarlet and orange and yellow – fiery colours for a fiery woman. She smiles and sulks. She sings to me like a nightingale. She dances with me in her arms, like a butterfly blown by the breeze.

Sometimes we are together in the garden at Hatfield Palace. I recognize the fountain. A grey dog yaps at her heels and she shows me how to pet him, but he snarls at me, nips my fingers with his little teeth. I dislike him because his panting breath stinks of the dark earth where he has scratched.

She picks up a peacock's feather from the gravel and tickles my neck. I giggle and snatch it from her, tickling under her chin. She arches her neck, laughing, and the emeralds sag. I drop the feather and scream, thinking that I have cut her skin, for there is a splash of crimson on her neck. My mother slaps my fingers as I touch it. Then she takes off my little satin shoes to dangle my bare feet in the cool water of the fountain and says, "Hush, *ma petite rose, ne pleure pas*...don't cry, it's only a

68

little strawberry mark," and I calm again, although I wonder why she wears a strawberry on her neck.

And every night, I thanked Francis for bringing me the box – and Alys for keeping her promise to my mother. Would my boast to Robert Dudley remain an idle one? How could *I* find Francis? Like Robert, I had never been away from any of my palaces alone, at night or by day.

Kat never spoke of the perfume that lingered on me. Instead, she brought me new perfumes to try, some floral, some fruity as if to mask the one that *she* had not chosen. Apple was her favourite. Sometimes she was so heavy-handed that wasps flew at my neck when I walked in the garden.

My mother lightened my heart. She took me back to innocent times. I saw the best in everybody about me.

I sparkled.

My skin brightened too. I asked for egg whites to be sent up from the kitchen every morning. I might have smelled like my mother, but I did not have to look like her. It is the only part of her that I dislike. I have inherited her sallow skin.

When you love somebody, there must be no secrets between you. So enthralled had I been by remembering my mother that I forgot that this alone would not tell me the truth about her.

Oh, the glimpses of my mother enchanted me, but they told me only what happened when we were together. They did not tell me what was happening in her dangerous world. In my heart, I wanted to believe that she was innocent. But doubts often overwhelmed me. I blamed too many years of gossip. *Was* the splash of strawberry red on her neck the mark of a witch? *Was* the dog her witch's familiar? As she played with me, *was* she already committing adultery?

I had to know.

I cursed myself for mocking Francis. He must have disguised himself to seek me out, I thought. He was well-spoken, of good breeding with his straight back and limbs. He was not used to such toil on the river – that was why his hands were ruined. Why had his servant not bathed them with comfrey? Why had he not bathed his sores with camomile?

 70

How could I speak to Francis now?

One thought consoled me. He *will* come back. Did I not command it on my birthday? People always do what I ask. I am a princess.

Then I let my thoughts run away with me, glorious thoughts of when I would meet Alys for the first time. Francis will take me to a beautiful country house where his mother and I will nibble sugared rose petals and marzipan fruits and sip honeyed milk and talk only of my mother.

What will it be like to talk to somebody who knew her? I asked myself. What will it be like to hear the truth from her lips?

Chapter Six

The rose heads had rotted and hardened into scarlet rose hips. The lavender had faded and its seed heads sagged under the weight of ceaseless autumn rain. On the first fine dawn, Kat and I resumed our morning rides along the river path, away from Chelsea, towards fields full of sodden stubble.

It was a bright October day, clouds scudding, wind releasing red-gold leaves and swirling them across the Thames. We took the river path, skirting Chelsea

Woods, until the sky darkened again and heavy rain forced us back the way we had come. Then a storm engulfed us.

Close to Chelsea Palace, we found the path blocked by a fallen oak and slippery with filthy water from the swollen Thames. I would have urged my horse to jump it, but Kat said we must return home through the woods.

We rode in single file, for the track was narrow. Impatient, I went ahead, anxious to be out of the damp gloom. A sharp gust of wind took off my riding hat and my hair coiled in the wet air. Branches bent and cracked as the storm deepened, letting through flashes of lightning, scattering sheltering deer. It would have been good hunting.

But I was the hunted.

A man ran from the trees, a gnarled-faced man in an old cloak. I thought nothing of it as he ran towards me. I am used to it. It is the part of being a princess that I like best, for I like to be recognized – even though I know that one day it might be somebody who bears me a grudge, somebody who might want to harm me. Lights glimmered in the trees and I thought there must be woodmen or charcoal burners sitting out the storm and one of them had come to offer his assistance.

"We heard the Boleyn bastard was riding today," the man called.

Too late, I recognized the smell that I knew from my sister Mary – the cloying scent of incense that is forbidden by the new faith. Too late, I saw the crucifix around his neck. I whipped the man away from me, but he risked death by clinging to my reins and staring deep into my eyes. "Look at your devil eyes," he hissed. "Just like the witch *she* was. Like mother, like daughter." At last, he let go.

My heart thudded in fearful rhythm to his vile words as I galloped across the waterlogged meadow, scattering poppy heads and calves, until we came to the back entrance of the palace. Thomas Seymour was there, ordering his servants and groomsmen.

"It seems that Lady Catherine's added another parrot to her menagerie," Kat said.

I smiled in spite of my distress, for my stepfather was wearing scarlet and green velvet and yellow hose to

match the feather in his cap. "An old parrot," I added. "He's almost forty, yet he struts like a young man."

Within seconds, Thomas Seymour was holding me around the waist and lifting me down as you would a child. "Ah, the wild women of the woods," he roared, laughing.

I was close to tears. "Not as wild as the men," I shouted. "Did you know there are Catholics living in the woods? They've made an altar in the trees and hung candles from the branches. How can you let them worship so close to your house? It's against the law."

"They were probably celebrating morning Mass when you rode by," he said. "They cause *us* no trouble. It's the sight of you that has inflamed them." He wiped mud from my cheek. "You would do that to any man, Bess. Your father gave up the old faith to marry your mother and they have never forgiven her." He could see that I was close to tears, but he did not spare me. "And they might never forgive you."

"One of them called me vile names," I said. "Words hurt. They enter your mind like maggots make their way into decaying flesh…"

Behind me, Kat tut-tutted at my choice of words. "Don't exaggerate," she said. "You're overtired." Her creased skin softened and flushed like a young girl's as she asked my stepfather where he was going.

"To Devon, Mistress Ashley, to inspect the King's navy. Look after Bess well, for I'll not be back before November."

I breathed deeply for the first time since my birthday. Tomorrow, I thought, and the day after...and the weeks after that...I can lie late in my bed.

We celebrated Jane's tenth birthday. Then my brother's, born a few days after her. Church bells pealed for him at dawn, waking Kat into a quarrelsome humour.

Lady Catherine was in fine spirits as we ate breakfast. "My three little autumn leaves," she said, laughing.

"Let's hope we don't fall like them," I said.

At noon, we journeyed to Whitehall Palace for Edward's celebrations. I loved my little brother, even though his mother had taken the place of mine. But it was not the same now that he was the King. Before, we

had played games. Now I could not turn my back on him when I left his presence chamber, but I had to walk backwards towards the door, which is very difficult to do. And it seemed unfair that he should sit on the throne first just because he was the prince. I sighed. Perhaps it was for the best. No Queen would be allowed to rule alone. She would be forced to take a husband to help her.

I was more nervous than usual as Kat helped me into the royal barge. I had not forgotten the man in the woods. Although it would be treason to call out such things in public and few would dare, I chose a waterside seat in the barge, away from the crowds, sinking into cushions that were soft and deep. Kat took the bank side, next to Lady Catherine. Jane sat opposite, with her nurse, Mistress Ellen.

The Thames was as smooth as glass, unlike the day I had first seen Francis. I had looked for him ever since, walking by the river although I hated its stench. But he never came back.

I sighed and Kat patted my hand.

The banks were bright with bunches of flowers and

wheat and garlands of autumn leaves – in celebration of the greatest harvest of all, a living prince. At Chelsea Village, there were crowds on the riverbanks, some dangling their feet in the water. People had left their apple-picking to see us. I bowed my head until a woman called out, "God bless you, Princess Elizabeth."

"They love you," Kat said. "Who could not?" And there was a tear on her cheek.

"You would make a fine Queen, Bess," my stepmother said. My heart swelled with love for her. I owed her everything. It was she who had persuaded my father to recognize Mary and me as his legitimate heirs. But in that love was guilt for wanting to know the truth about my mother.

I leaned past Kat and waved back.

"What was it like to be the Queen of England?" Jane asked.

"Oh…exciting….exhausting…and dangerous," Lady Catherine said. "A Queen must have the weak and feeble body of a woman, while being strong enough to bear sons – that is what the King wants – but she must have the mind of a man. A Queen must never draw attention

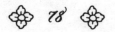

to herself. There is a line that must not be crossed. The problem is this: it is an invisible line. *You* have to find out where it is. I once crossed it, and it almost cost me my head."

Jane gasped. "*You?*" she said, astonished. "But you are the most... What did you do?"

"I was said to be too extreme in my religious views."

"*Were* you?" Jane's eyes bulged.

"Perhaps," she replied. "But I do not think that my views were the problem. It was the fact that I was seen to be more outspoken than my husband. The Bishop of Winchester told Henry that he had found banned religious books in my library. Your father signed my arrest..." She shivered. "I would have been taken to the Tower. By chance, I heard about it."

Mistress Ellen was aghast. "So what did you do then, madam?"

"I took to my bed and pretended to be ill...*very* ill... and wept and begged Henry to forgive me. And he did. I still don't know why. He had mellowed with age, I suppose. But you can see how much men rule our lives."

"Bess becomes ill when she's in trouble," Kat said. "But she doesn't pretend. She swells up like a pig's bladder. If she fell into this river, she'd float."

Jane suddenly laughed and could not stop until she hiccoughed. But her whole body trembled.

We settled into silence, smiling at the chatter of Mistress Ellen and Kat as they recalled their girlhoods in Devon, the old faith, the old ways and the old days of perpetual sun.

Two miles downriver, we passed the turreted and gilded towers of Whitehall Palace. This was the palace my father had built for my mother and my longing for her rushed at me like the water beneath us. We did not stop there yet, for we were first to pick up Robert Dudley and his brother, Guildford. Further into London, we passed Edward Seymour's new house, still half-built. Garlands of cream and green ivy dangled from the wooden scaffold right to the rooftop. Then we came to Durham House, the London residence of the Dudley family.

Guildford Dudley was a year or two older than Jane, sulky-mouthed and flabby-skinned. He and Robert sat at the prow of the barge, beyond the canopy. Robert turned to shout, "Jane, I thought that if the King didn't marry you, Guildford might."

Jane pressed her lips tight. "I shall never marry."

"Then he might do for you, Bess?"

"I think not. You know that I don't want to marry either. Look what happened to my mother."

Robert laughed, uneasy. "Brother, we're in the presence of two unwise virgins."

Jane blushed. Kat tut-tutted. Mistress Ellen called, "Watch your words, sir, or I'll wash your mouth out with water."

"Not this water, I hope, madam," he shouted back, "for I'd not live long enough to annoy you again."

As we approached the water steps of Whitehall Palace, the oarsmen slowed and turned abruptly, cursing as they almost collided with a small rowing boat.

Jane screamed.

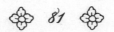 *81*

We all looked down, permitting us a sight that I shall never forget, the sight of a corpse being hauled into the boat – the corpse of a young woman, belly big with child, her head flung back so that she seemed to gaze up at us with horror-struck eyes. I followed the arch of her swollen body. Torrents of muddy water gushed from her mouth.

Mistress Ellen put her hand over Jane's eyes and Kat's hands were raised to mine, but I pushed them away. Lady Catherine made the sign of the cross. We all did.

I knew the boat. I knew the boy in it. I knew the strange woollen hat.

He was Francis.

"Charon," I mumbled.

Guildford spoke at last. "Who's he?" he asked. His voice still lisped like a child's.

"He's the ferryman in hell," Jane explained, still crying. "He rows the souls of the dead across the rivers of the underworld to the Elysian Fields...well...to paradise. That's why the Ancient Greeks placed a golden coin in the mouths of their dead. Otherwise, the ferryman wouldn't take them."

Dreadful thoughts raced through my mind. I had believed Francis to be a gentleman in disguise, but no gentleman would do this death work. The hands that had touched my mother's perfume box were tainted with death. Yet, in the midst of the horror, I was relieved. Francis *was* real. I had not dreamed him any more than I had dreamed the perfume box. Now I knew where to find him.

But how would I ever be able to speak to him?

Robert Dudley leaned over the barge rail, shaking his fist, cursing, "Do your death work somewhere else!" he shouted. "It's the King's birthday today."

"Somebody has to do it," Francis called back. "Do you think you could take your fancy barges up and down the river if I didn't? Anyway, the dead don't care for celebrations."

The front oarsman shouted, "Doff your cap to the King's mother and sister." He reached over, pulled off the woollen hat, and Francis's hair sprang out, as red and as gold as mine. He quickly snatched the hat back, sat down with his companion and rowed towards London Bridge.

And I sank into sombre thoughts.

If Francis truly earned his living in this way, did Alys live in a rat-filled hovel somewhere on the river? If she did, then there would be no rose petals and marzipan and honeyed milk for me. Well, I would face it for my mother's sake. I would take fresh lavender in my pomander.

It was a sad party that greeted Edward at the water steps of Whitehall Palace. My heart turned over at the sight of his serious little face. Poor Edward – whom I could no longer scoop into my arms and smother with kisses, because he was now the King. He was peevish at the sight of our wretched faces. He commanded us to be cheerful for his birthday.

"Ah – the little lion cub is sharpening his claws," Robert said. "Make sure he doesn't sink them into you, Bess."

"He's my brother," I replied. "We would *never* hurt each other."

I brightened as we entered his palace. I still missed the fun of living at court. Women are not permitted to live there if the King is not married.

I slipped away to the portrait gallery later that afternoon. I wanted to see my portrait again, the one I had had painted for my father the year before he died. I wanted to see how much I had changed.

The gallery at Whitehall Palace is as vast as Chelsea Palace. It is like walking in a summer garden, for its rush matting is always strewn with lavender and rose petals.

I had not entered it since my brother's coronation in February. *His* portrait now hung where my father's used to be. It was not the portrait of a King. That had not been painted yet. This was the profile of Edward when his cheeks still had the softness of childhood.

My portrait hung at his left hand. I was nearly thirteen when it had been painted. How sombre my face was. How innocent my eyes were. My glorious hair was restrained by a pearl-studded headdress. Pearls adorned my ears and my fingers. They circled my waist on a thin girdle, and my neck on the three-pearled pendant that matched Lady Catherine's. The artist had taken great care. There was nothing in it that could have reminded my father of my mother.

My shoulders are so thin, I thought. They remind me of Jane's. I have a woman's body now, but I know that my eyes have not lost their innocence. Is this what Thomas Seymour sees?

At Edward's right hand hung Mary, painted three years ago when she was twenty-eight, sweet-faced and fashionable in rich crimson velvet and brocade, rubies at her neck.

We're all the King's pups, I thought, but none from the same litter.

Then I noticed. Above Mary hung a portrait of her mother, Catherine of Aragon. Above Edward hung a portrait of his mother, Jane Seymour. My father had given up my spirited dark-eyed mother for her prissy smile so that he might have a son.

And above me? A blank wall.

I made my way to Lady Catherine, who had entered the gallery at the far end. She stood, head bowed and I think she might have been offering a prayer, for she stood in front of a portrait of my father when he was eighteen or nineteen. He was handsome and straight and strong-limbed.

"I wish I had known your father as a young man," she said, "before he had to be carried to his throne on a chair."

I had seen this portrait many times when I had come to court. But now I saw it differently. It confirmed what I should have already seen, something I did not want to see. Take away the sores. Take away the woollen hat. Take away the grime. Imagine a red-gold beard and it could have been Francis's portrait hanging there. He was more like my father than the two bastard sons he had already recognized: Henry Blount, who had died at the age of seventeen, and my cousin Henry, the son of my mother's sister. And more like my father than my brother Edward, eating marzipan downstairs.

My head swam.

Had I taken a gift from somebody who might be my brother? Never take gifts from a stranger, for there is always a price to pay. Or was it poison – a poison so slow that even now it was secretly destroying me? Was it a plot to remove me from the succession? Was it a Catholic conspiracy between Francis and my sister Mary? A bastard son can be dangerous. Everybody

knows that. He can demand the throne of England if he dares and gather people around him to help.

Shock made me slow-witted as we returned to the King's chambers. Francis was my only path to the truth about my mother. But if he *was* my father's son, how could I hear the truth from a woman who must have been my father's mistress? Of course I knew that my father had had mistresses, but for Alys to have borne his child… Could I trust her? A mother will do anything for her son. Was my mother's perfume a bribe from Alys for her son's rightful name?

Warm wine and sugar restored everybody's spirits but mine. For the return journey to Durham House, Dudley and Guildford squeezed inside the canopy with us for the wind was spotted with rain. Robert and I were awkward with each other, as if we knew that the games of childhood were over.

We fell silent at the spot where we had seen Francis.

"That's the boy I want you to find," I said softly, cupping my hand around Robert's ear. "Now I need to find him more than ever. There's something I want to ask him, something he hasn't told me." I did not mention

the likeness to my father and it was clear that Robert had not noticed it.

He cursed under his breath. "I can't imagine what a broken creature the mother must be if her son has to fish bodies from the river," he said.

"*Please*, Robert."

"No. Keep away from him. He's trouble."

"It's rude to whisper," my stepmother said.

We did not speak again. My dreams of sugared rose petals and honeyed milk and sweet talk with Alys had faded as quickly as the autumn light.

Mistress Ellen broke the silence. Her eyes gleamed in the grey light. "I'll tell you a sorry tale," she began. "The Second Henry, like all Kings, had a mistress with skin and hair as pale as first snow, so beautiful that she was called Fair Rosamund. She bore the King two children…"

My heart plummeted. The sight of Francis that afternoon had unnerved me. I was in no mood for tales of Kings and their mistresses. I glared at Mistress Ellen, willing the barge to lurch and make her sick. But she was determined to entertain us.

89

"When he married, his wife Eleanor was so mad with jealousy that Henry built a palace for Rosamund, hidden deep inside a maze," Mistress Ellen went on. "Only he knew the way. Eleanor sent servants to find it, but they never came back."

I looked across at Jane and Guildford. They sat perfectly still, their faces pale in the reflection of the water.

"One night, Henry caught his foot in the hem of Rosamund's night robe and when he left her, he unwound a silver thread like the silvery trail of a snail…"

"Like the silver thread of the Thames," I snapped, trying to hurry the story to its conclusion. "And it led Eleanor to her husband's mistress."

Kat was angry. "Let her spin out her tale, Bess."

"No, it's told now," Mistress Ellen said. She scowled at me.

"I'll finish it then," Kat said. "Eleanor followed the glittering thread, past hissing snakes and biting spiders, past trees that had pleated overhead, past the skeletons of her dead servants…" Robert tapped his foot against mine and pulled a gruesome face. But I could not laugh.

"…until she came to a pink castle where Fair Rosamund was combing her glorious hair. Eleanor held up a dagger and a cup of poison. 'How do you want to die?' she asked."

My body swayed.

"Dagger," Robert said.

"Poison," Jane shouted.

"I'll finish," Mistress Ellen cut in. "Fair Rosamund drank from the poisoned cup and fell to the floor – dead."

My throat tightened. This is how I shall die, I thought. The perfume is already seeping into my skin and slowly killing me.

"On her tomb, they carved: *Here lies a rose not pure. She, the once-perfumed wench, now yields no perfume, but a stench.*" Kat shrieked in triumph.

I screamed. I blamed the water, suddenly swelling in a sharp gust of wind that brought in dying leaves from the garlanded banks.

But Kat was warming to her audience. "It's an east wind," she warned. "We used to call it devil's breath. Soon he'll attack with greater force."

"And when will that be, Kat?" Robert asked, touching my ankle with his foot.

"On All Hallows Eve, of course," she said, "when the souls of the dead rattle at the windows to speak to us. It used to be a night for good, when we rang the church bells to help the dead on their way through purgatory to heaven. Now it's a night when you wouldn't want to step outside, for fear the devil will tread on your toes."

"What will they do now that Edward has abolished purgatory?" Jane asked.

"I don't know. Has the King told all these wandering souls?" Robert asked. "They might be surprised to find themselves homeless."

They laughed. And so he cheered and charmed them all. But I felt only deep dread...felt the poison mingle with my blood. The sight of Francis in his death boat, the drowned girl, the portrait of my father, all conspired to fill my mind with gruesome thoughts of danger and death.

Thomas Seymour had returned from Devon, raging like a sea storm. "A devil of a job John Dudley has passed on to me," he grumbled. "We need to build more ships if England's to defend herself against invasion. Our fine forests will have to be chopped."

"What will our Catholics do then?" I asked.

He shrugged. "They'll go deeper and deeper into the woods until they become pixies. If they don't, they'll face the flames."

"Faith should keep us alive, not dead," I said.

"Wise Bess," he murmured. He stared hard at me. "The river's brought a bloom to your cheeks. Or was it Robert Dudley? Take care, my little rose. John Dudley will do anything for power. He'll marry one of his sons to any woman who inherits the throne...after Edward."

"Do you wish my brother dead, sir? That smacks of treason."

"No, but he hasn't got your father's strong constitution. Your Robert Dudley might marry Mary, if she succeeds to the throne."

"Then he will taste blood on her lips. Didn't you once pursue her yourself?"

"Cruel Bess."

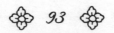 93

"I was wise just now."

"Cruel. Wise. Moderate in faith." He laughed. "Yes, just as a Queen should be… Or a wife."

"Lock my bedchamber door tonight, Kat," I said.

"But, child, you hate to be shut in."

"The devil might come in."

"The devil doesn't use doors," she replied. "He slips through chinks and cracks and you might not recognize him, for he comes in many disguises."

"Lock it anyway," I snapped.

I was lavish with my mother's perfume that night. I needed her protection against a world that had turned as black as the moonless night.

She is thinner than before and I am plumper. Yet her belly is swollen. She tugs my little hands towards it and her sleeves fall back and on the left hand, next to her little finger, is another finger, half-grown, squirming like a maggot, and I laugh and touch it so that it squiggles again, and as she leans over her belly her ribbon hangs loose from her neck, and I see the scarlet mark again that I saw before and she is whispering, "Soon, you shall have a brother, sweet Bess, and it will save my life."

The sight of her frightens me. *Boleyn witch*, the man in the woods had called her.

I snapped the lid of the perfume box tight and pressed the bone by the side of my little finger. Then I searched my neck for moles and warts and felt between my breasts for a third nipple.

The devil *did* enter my bedchamber. This devil had a key. He must have taken off his shoes as the swordsman did when he approached my mother. I only felt his devil's breath on my neck. I only heard the rustle of his sleeve as he touched my hair so lightly that it could have been no more than a moth, and his words no more than a dreamed whisper: "Oh, your mother was enchanting… you smell just like her…" Then: "They said that may blossom drifted onto your mother's head," he suddenly whispered, "lighting up her raven hair like pearls and as she prepared to leave this world, she took one and smelled it. And all the time, not a sound, from her or the crowd. Not one petal fell onto the swordsman or the sword, only onto her."

Between sleep and waking, with her thin face still fresh in my mind, I burst into tears. "Everybody is willing to speak of her death," I cried. "But nobody will speak of her life."

He put his arm around my shoulders. I stiffened, confused. Oh, he was cunning. So silent, so gentle, that he made me think I was dreaming and in my half-sleep I moved towards him, until I remembered.

I screamed for Kat and she came running almost at once, drawing back the bed curtains, letting in the dull dawn. She scolded Seymour. He tried to charm her with jest and tickles, but when she threatened to tell Lady Catherine, he soured. "Cease your noise, madam," he roared. "I have done nothing wrong."

"Think of your daughter's reputation, sir," she pleaded.

"*Hers?*" he roared. "It seems I must think of my own, since I stand accused of…I know not what. What *are* you accusing me of, Mistress Ashley?" She eyed the bunch of keys, but dared not say more. "I am innocent,"

my stepfather shouted. "And if you continue with this slander, I shall tell my brother the Protector, and he will punish you for it."

He left without bowing to either of us.

"There speaks a guilty man," Kat said. "If you are truly innocent, there is no need to say so."

The days darkened. Mid-winter imprisoned us with bitter winds and dark fogs. They lowered my spirits, made me brood on the last few weeks.

I had trusted Francis. Now it seemed that he had not told me the truth about himself. Had he plotted to lure me to a hovel on the riverbank where my life would swiftly end, bringing him one step closer to the throne of England? Perhaps his mother knew nothing of it. Yet *who* had warned Francis to hide his hair under that ridiculous hat so that nobody would see the resemblance to my father?

When my thoughts torment me, as they have done since childhood, I turn to music and dancing. My spirits rose at the thought of Christmastide.

We would go to Greenwich Palace, a small palace on the south bank of the Thames, built to receive visitors who sailed into Gravesend from Europe. This is where my father was born and died. This is where I was born. It is my favourite palace.

Then, too late, I remembered. It would be a sombre celebration: no music, no dancing, no gambling, no cockfights or bear baiting, for it would almost be the first anniversary of my father's death.

Well, I would wear white and silver again for Robert Dudley and we would dance together in our minds.

Chapter Seven

"You should not be living with a woman who has dishonoured our father's name," Mary protested. Her deep voice carried to the painted ceiling. "You should have come to live with me when I invited you. Living with her will damage your reputation."

"But Mary, Lady Catherine is one of your closest friends. Don't you miss her?"

She shook her head.

It *had* been a sombre Christmastide at Greenwich

Palace. On this last and twelfth night, people were quarrelsome after so long together without their usual distractions. Robert Dudley, ill with a fever, had already gone home.

"She has betrayed our father's memory by marrying so soon after his death and without the King's permission," Mary went on. "That is treason. And if she had been with child, whose baby would it have been?" She flopped like an overblown rose in her red damask dress and rubies. Together we made a true Tudor rose, the white against the red.

"But she isn't, so it doesn't matter," I said. "Our little brother wants her to be happy."

"But he does not want *me* to be happy," she complained. "He forbids me so much – my rosary, my Mass, my crucifix." She winced. Looking down, I saw that she clutched her crucifix: so encrusted with rubies that Christ's blood seemed to seep from her hand. "And he expects me to eat in the same room as *him*." She looked towards Thomas Cranmer, the Archbishop of Canterbury, seated in the corner of the room. "Do you know why his cheeks are so plump for such an old man?"

"No. Does he eat too much?"

"The devil lives inside his mouth and speaks for him. He mocks God's mystery."

"No, Mary, he makes God's words plain for all to understand," I replied. "Thanks to him, people will soon be able to read the *Book of Common Prayer* in English instead of Latin… Well…those who can read."

Now Mary frowned at me as she had frowned every day for the twelve days of Christmastide, even when we had exchanged gifts. She had grown sadder and stouter in the months since Edward's coronation. She must have been at a forbidden Mass, for her faded auburn hair gave off the smell of incense, like the man in Chelsea Woods.

"And *you* are different," she said. "I liked you best before."

"Before *what*?"

"Before you grew to look like…*her*…that woman who stole my father from my mother. I have been watching you this last week. When you laugh and flash your eyes, men – I mean, Robert Dudley…Thomas Seymour – come running. Do they come running for me? No. *Jamás.* I am too kind, too gentle. I—"

Anger feeds upon anger. Now I spoke with equal rage. "Do you think that men want to kiss a woman whose lips reek constantly of God's blood?" I cried. "Why don't you pray to God as we do? And – perhaps you've forgotten? – my mother has a name. She's called Anne. Anne Boleyn. She was the Queen of England and she gave birth to me *here*."

Behind us, Thomas Seymour was chuckling.

"I know. I was there... A princess of seventeen, forced to watch my father's *puta*..." She broke off, crying, and ran from the Great Hall.

"*In vino veritas*," my stepfather said. "It seems that she's drunk on God's blood."

Concerned, I followed Mary up the staircase into the gloom of the first floor, into my birthing room: the Chamber of the Wise Virgins. The pungent smell of camphor hit me. Dust dulled the curtains and the bright colours of the tapestries.

My father had wanted no wise virgin daughter, but a son.

 *102*

I gave up the Pope for this, he had said.

Mary had lifted a small candle from the wall bracket outside the door. Now it lit a chair, a table and an enormous bed, shrouded with purple silk – the bed where my mother had laboured for many hours. I had seen it many times, but the sight still tightened my throat.

My sister was clutching her stomach. She had not seen me behind her. "It was here that the *puta* spawned her daughter, Elizabeth – *infanta del diablo* – and I was forced to watch its birth and if I had the chance I would have snuffed out its life…" I had never heard such words spill from her lips and I hoped that I had misunderstood her Spanish. She paused to open a small velvet bag, to take out a piece of lace; a narrow bottle; a lock of hair.

Her relics. Her past.

"The whore sold her body to sit on the throne of *Inglaterra*; but she sat there for only three years…"

I stood spellbound. Yet my heart filled with pity for her, for her mother had died only months before mine. "Maria, Maria," I called softly. Her voice trailed away. I went and embraced her gently, felt her bones under my fingers. "Hush, Mary. What's made you to speak like this tonight? You've never blamed me for…what my mother did."

"The sight of *you*," she spat.

She pulled the stopper from the bottle and held it to my nose. I recoiled. "It is poison," she whispered, "like the one that turned my mother's heart black, that poor heart that loved your father too much." She forced the bottle to my nostrils. It reeked of filthy water. "The witch whore sent it to her. I never saw my mother before she died. That witch would not permit it."

I stroked her hand, full of pity for her ravaged face. Then I gently pushed the bottle away. "Mary, we both know what it's like to be called bastards, and neglected because we were not princes," I said. "We both have mothers whose lives were in danger from the moment they gave birth to daughters…and we both let our mothers rule us from the grave."

"How could our mothers be the *same*?" she spat at me. She held up the slender candle to my face. "You think that the crown will sit upon your head, sister, if dear Edward dies, just because you share the same faith. But it will be *mine*. I have worn Christ's crown of thorns

all my adult life and my head throbs with pain. My grandmother was the Queen of Spain. My mother was the Queen of England. I shall be *Maria Regina*. You are a *bastarda*." She hissed the word. "That whore was never married to my father. *She* signed a document to confess it… *She* made you a *bastarda*."

I ceased to hear any more. It was not the last word that took my breath away – I had been declared illegitimate after my mother's death – but I did not know that my own mother had signed away my name.

"No…no…no…" I muttered.

"Oh, *si, si, si*," she shouted, triumphant. Her voice hissed like the candle. "In God's eyes, you will always be a *bastarda*. GO. Go and hide away in the dark."

I went straight to Archbishop Cranmer. "Please, Your Grace, help me," I whispered.

As he laid his hands on my head, his voluminous sleeves enclosed me like heavenly clouds. I let my body soften. "God is here, child," he intoned. "He is helping you."

I removed his hands, held them so tight that he

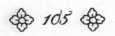

winced. "I need *your* help," I insisted. I had never dared to question him about my mother. "You were with my mother in the Tower at her last communion. Did she say anything about me?"

"She spoke to God, not to me."

"Your Grace, you are my godfather. Tell me the truth. Did she sign anything before she died?"

He avoided my desperate eyes. "I was shocked by the accusations against her," he said.

"I don't mean that." My voice rose. His attendants closed in, but he waved them back. "The old faith keeps man in a state of awe and ignorance. The new faith lets us hear the truth with our own ears, not a priest's. You are translating our prayer book from Latin into English so that soon everybody can understand what happens when we pray. Yet you cannot tell me the truth. It is a simple question: did she sign away my royal name?"

He glanced at my brother, who was taking his place at the head of the table, his lopsided shoulders scarcely supporting his head with its heavy crown.

"I...I can't..." He began to gently push me away from him with his foot, as you do a beggar.

 *106*

"Take care, Your Grace, let me make it as plain as your prayer book. My brother looks unwell tonight, don't you think? He often does. And my poor tutor, Master Grindal, burns with fever. What will you do when my sister Mary sits on the throne? Do you think she will forgive you, banning her Mass, smashing her statues and saints, forcing her followers into the woods? She will have those trees chopped down to make your wood pile and you will burn on Tower Hill long before you get to hell."

His attendants would have handled me as roughly as a common beggar, but he signalled them to leave me, as he did. "May God protect you, Your Grace," he whispered, "and lead you to the truth."

Only Alys could do that. But without Francis, I did not know where she was. And if I found out, could I trust her now? Or did she seek to put her son on the throne of England?

Chapter Eight

I went down to the river, watching the winter's day deepen into dusk from the water steps. Usually this is my favourite time of the year, when all is icy sheen on land and water. The Thames shimmered under its thin crust of ice. Beyond, barges jostled for space at the moorings, their bargemen huddled over warming ale.

The Romans called it Tamesis, the dark river. In my mind it was now the river of the dead.

The clouds thinned and parted. A full moon spilled

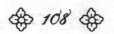

its glorious light onto the water. I fancied that the moon was my mother's head floating free. She used to look at me with love and kiss me all the time and cool my feet in the fountain...I remember it all now...so why did she choose, at the last moment, to annul her marriage to my father and leave me without a royal name?

I stared into the glittering water that could take me to Alys, taking care not to fall in, for I knew that the weight of my furs would drag me down to the mud. *She* could tell me the secrets of my mother's soul, as no perfume could.

"It wouldn't be worth the trouble of throwing yourself in, for I'd pull you out," a voice said. It was a gentle voice with a French accent. "It would be rich pickings for me though – a Princess."

So silently had his little boat drifted to the water steps that I smelled Francis before I saw him – the stench of death and decay that I had smelled when I first met him. He held up his lantern with bare hands that were clawed with cold. His pinched face flared with sores.

"The river always gives up its dead, however long it takes," he said. "And when you float to the surface your

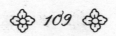

body's bloated with stinking water and your eye sockets scuttle with crabs…"

Part of me had longed to see him again, for nobody but his mother could tell me what I wanted to know. And part of me was consumed by anger that he had dared to show his face again. I glanced towards the guards at the top of the water steps. They would not move unless I commanded them, although they watched my every move. "If you do not tell me who you really are, I shall have you arrested now," I said. "I only have to shout *one* word – *treason* – and they'll take you to the Tower."

"Shout it then, if that's what you want." His lantern rattled as the boat bobbed. Francis looked as wretched as those he pulled from the water.

I leaned towards him, straining to be heard above the noise of the bargemen. "So is it true? *Are* you my father's natural son?" I wanted him to deny it.

"Yes. Does it matter?"

"Of course it does. It smacks of conspiracy."

He raised his eyebrows. "Is it a conspiracy when a woman sacrifices her own reputation for the woman she

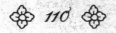

serves?" he asked. "Do you know that a man can't lie with his wife when she's with child? It's against the church's teaching."

Could he see my blush in the near-darkness? "Of course I do," I said, although I did not know it.

"That's when men often take mistresses, especially kings. When your mother was with child – with you – your mother chose mine to lie with your father until you were born. It's common practice. For your father, this was almost the same as being faithful to your mother. For her, it was a way of keeping her husband close by."

"So we are almost the same age? I thought that…"

"I look older," he replied "It's the life I've been forced to lead."

My rage quietened. I sank to the steps, deep in thought. Icy water seeped into my velvet shoes. How much wiser Francis seemed than me. How little I understood of the world and the way it worked.

"When my mother found herself with child, just before your birth, your mother sent her to friends in France," he went on. "She left me there to come back to court. She didn't expect your mother to die so soon, not when your father...our father...loved her so much."

"Was your mother with her when she died?"

"Oh, yes. But she could not bear to stay here afterwards. She was afraid of protesting your mother's innocence too much. She would have done it – but for me. So she returned to France and we lived on the kindness of friends until your father died."

This talk of our mothers was so natural, so welcome that it soothed me. Longing for mine washed over me like the water at my feet. What would I give to talk to Alys for an hour, a minute, a second?

"Where does your mother live, Francis?" I asked. "Is it far?" I smiled at him for the first time.

He was lost for words. I tried to help him, sensing that he was ashamed of his poverty. "It does not matter if you live in a simple cottage or worse, a hovel in the mud... Kat could fill my pomander with fresh lavender and—"

Francis laughed, the lusty laugh of my father, and so loud that one of the guards moved forward. Then he began to mutter, as if to himself. "Nothing can prepare you for what you'll see and hear. The devil is King *there*…" His voice faltered. I thought that shame still stopped him from naming some wretched place.

"Where is she, Francis?"

He might have struck me with his oar, for he whispered a word so foul that it stopped my breath.

He whispered, "Bedlam."

Had I misheard? My heart thudded. Who had not heard of Bedlam – St Bethlehem's Hospital for lunatics, by Bishops Gate in London Wall, where poor souls shrieked and cried the devil's nonsense day and night?

Pity drained from me. I was the one who shrieked. "So you've chosen to mock me, Francis, like the man in the woods, like Jane, like Mary. You're as steeped in spite as they are. You've preyed on my longing for my mother, just because you couldn't know your father. It's —"

"Listen to me —"

"*Listen*? I've listened all my life and what have I heard? Lies. And now – more lies." I stamped my foot, cursing. "Cranmer won't tell me the truth. My stepfather won't, although he tempts me with titbits. I thought your mother would."

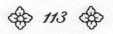

"She *will*…"

"How can she, when she's lost her wits?"

"Listen. Bedlam's full of women who must be silenced because they're seen to be troublesome," he said. "There are wives who accuse their husbands of being unfaithful, and daughters who accuse their fathers of…lewd acts. Yes, put such women in Bedlam and they're silenced. Let them shriek and shout all day and rattle their chains all night and nobody listens. Don't you understand? You can speak the truth in Bedlam and nobody believes it."

"Are you saying that your mother isn't mad?"

"Yes…although it's a wonder she isn't, with the sights she's seen. We came back from France after your father died last year, to offer you the silver box, to offer you the truth. But my mother reckoned without *her* father. He feared that she'd bring shame to the family by seeking you out, by speaking out. *He* put her in Bedlam – her own father! He refused to recognize me as his grandson. So I fend for myself. This is why I work like this, to earn money to take us back to France."

"Do you expect me to believe you?" I moaned. "It isn't fair. It isn't fair."

"No, it isn't. She's in Bedlam because of *you*."

I did not know what to believe. It is in this way that plots are skilfully woven. Each thread is so perfect that its subtleties cannot always be seen. If this *was* a plot to bring me down, then Bedlam was the supreme deception. Devious, designed to mislead. If I entered its dreadful doors, I might swiftly disappear.

"So, do you still want to speak to her?" he asked.

I have many weaknesses – my temper, my dropsy, my impatience – but it is my reluctance to make decisions that plagues me more than anything else. If I did not have maidservants to dress me, I would stay in my night robe all day. If I must make a decision, I put it off. Kat is driven insane by it.

My heart thudded with sudden panic. How could *I* go to Bedlam? Such things are impossible for princesses. How could I escape Kat's eyes? How could I escape other prying eyes? Bedlam was more than two miles from Chelsea Palace. I saw danger everywhere: in the dark river that could take me to hell or to my death, in my sister's hatred, in Seymour's fingers across my neck.

I wanted to be safe in the pink palace behind me

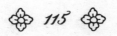 *115*

with Kat and Lady Catherine and Robert Dudley. As I pondered it all, a long shadow fell across me. Oars creaked in the icy darkness and the wash of Francis's boat lapped against the steps as he pushed away.

Francis had seen my stepfather, who was snatching a fire torch from the guard to hold over the water. "Who is that boy?" he asked me. He wrinkled his nose. "I can smell his stench from here."

"Nobody."

"I'm not a fool, Bess. Princesses don't talk to stinking boys in stinking boats. Kate has told me about such a boy…the one you saw on your brother's birthday. Is he another pup mewling for its master?"

"What do you mean?"

"I mean, Kate says he has the look of your father. London is full of such pups, claiming to be his son. They should be drowned at birth." Thomas Seymour took me by the arm and pulled me to my feet. My legs barely supported me as he led me towards the fire brazier to warm me. "Look at you, child. You're angry. You're distressed. What has he said? Tell me his name and I can warn him off. Princesses are easy prey, Bess."

For just one moment, I was tempted. I wanted to trust my stepfather. I wished that I did not feel so alone. But I knew how Thomas Seymour would warn Francis – with the mud at the bottom of the Thames. If I gave up Francis now, I would never hear the truth about my mother.

He touched my cheek. "Who is he, Bess?"

"Nobody," I insisted.

We returned to the warmth of the Great Hall. I was still shivering with shock. Jane lent me her gloves. Kat brought me dry shoes. Edward was waiting, drumming his thin fingers on the table. Mary was already seated at his right hand. My chair waited empty, at his left. I sank into it, shaking with cold, cursing that I had missed my chance a second time.

"All my children gathered together," Lady Catherine said.

"An ill-assorted trinity, *no*?" Mary snapped, her voice cold.

My face must have been terrible to see, for Mary whispered her apologies and blamed the wine. But my

distress brought no other comment. It was nothing unusual. Twelve days of cramped chambers, stale air and over-indulgence had made us all red-eyed and irritable.

The Twelfth Night cake was brought in towards ten o'clock. It was a masterpiece. Baked in the shape of the palace, it gleamed with gilded marzipan. As tradition required, a pea and a bean had been hidden inside. Whoever found the bean would be King of Twelfth Night. Whoever found the pea, would be his Queen. As tradition also required, Edward spat the bean from his mouth to loud cheers. The pea dropped from Mary's mouth as she ate, but she did not even feel it. Forbidden to carry the rosary beads of the old faith, they had been sewn into the folds of her underskirt and as she touched them, her face took on the rapture that you feel when you scratch a flea bite.

The pea rolled along the table. Jane could have caught it, but she shrank back. So could I. I tried, but it slipped through my numbed fingers and into the gaping mouth of Edward's spaniel.

A fitting end to a vile Christmastide – a dog on the throne of England.

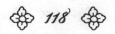

❋ ❋ ❋

Kat undressed me. "Thank the Lord. I shall sleep in my own bed tomorrow night," she said.

And I in mine, I thought. But how shall I sleep with Thomas Seymour prowling like a thief in the night?

Mary. Francis. Their so-called truths robbed me of sleep. Only fatigue stopped me hurling the perfume box from my window into the Thames. I used it instead, although there was little left.

The fragrance brought back the memory of my mother as it always did. I am here at Greenwich. I recognize the twin towers of the tilt yard. There is no frost. The air is scented with may blossom drifting down onto my mother's hair as she leans from the window to watch the joust. I can feel the wild beating of her heart when she holds me out to my father. It is the first time I have seen them together, the first time I have seen my father when he was young and strong – and there is little doubt that Francis is his son. He smiles at me. He shouts at her. Then they tug me, each taking an arm and a leg, almost splitting me from top to toe.

 119

My father leaves suddenly and her tears splash onto my face like spring rain. They run along my little nose and into my mouth and I do not like the salty taste and soon I am crying with her and I bury my face in her fragrant hair that smells of her perfume. Her body reeks of fear, rank and sour.

"What a pity I shall not live to see you bloom," she whispers.

The memory fades. And my tears flow so fast that the Thames should have burst its banks that night.

I slept late and when I came to breakfast, Mary had already left for Essex. We too made our way back by river to Chelsea Palace, on the silver water that could have taken me to Alys – and to the truth.

We were all out of spirits. It was a tiresome journey. A boat rowed in front of us to break the ice, but our progress was slow and chilling. A biting wind whistled through the canopy and chunks of ice struck the side of our barge. Of Francis, there was no sign. It was too cold for him to ply his deadly trade.

Once more, I regretted losing my temper with Francis. Anger is a brief madness, Lady Catherine said. It takes away our reason.

Chapter Nine

I entered my own Bedlam of writhing limbs and shrieking lips. My hands and feet swelled, then my whole body. Dropsy fills the body with water, although no one knows why. Kat did not call a physician, for I could not bear leeches to suck at my skin. I took to my bed.

Kat allowed no visitors, for Master Grindal had died of sweating sickness during Christmastide. A hush settled over the house. Everybody knew that the sweating sickness was swift of foot. You could dine at noon and die at dusk.

The strangest dream haunted me. My mother is there, young and laughing, holding the hand of a young man with eyes as dark as hers. She calls him her brother. But I am not a chubby child, as I am in my perfume memories; but the age I am now, with frightened face and hesitant step, trying to keep up with them as we walk in near darkness. My mother hands out apples and pears and bread to bony fingers poking through bars. It must be a prison, for there are many in London.

When I woke up, my eyes bulged like Jane's, and my belly heaved at the memory of a stench so strong that Kat came running with a bowl.

Illness left me weak in mind and body. I burst into tears if the maids stared at me. I was quarrelsome. I would not speak to Jane or to Lady Catherine.

Melancholia is a prison. It shuts you in, without a window to the world. It distorts your thoughts. I forget my mother's loving smile and soft words, remembering only her witch's marks and her hand with its wriggling finger.

Virgil says that the way to hell is easy. Its gates are open day and night. But to find the way back to fresh air is hard toil.

He is right. Sometimes, I hated Francis for dangling the truth in front of me, like a grown-up teases a child with a toy and moves away and away until the child cries and gives up. I plotted my revenge. I *would* denounce him to the King. I *would* have him taken to the Tower. Sometimes I pitied him. Sometimes I pitied Alys, sent to Bedlam because she had come back to England to keep her promise to my mother. More often than not, I pitied myself.

The day came when I was strong enough to walk in the garden with Kat. I kept well away from the river. From the rose walk, I could see there was only ice on the water, like the ice in the wind on my face – and in my heart.

Roger Ascham rode in from Cambridge. I watched him dismount, bright-skinned, hair and beard curly. I had begged my stepmother to secure him as my new tutor because he is said to have one of the cleverest minds in England. Now I wished him back in Cambridge because I was not in the mood for study.

"Master Ascham says your books will make you better," Kat said.

"What does *he* know?"

"More than you," she said with great patience. "Get up, Bess. You begged him to be your tutor. You must welcome him and dazzle him with your mind."

"I have no mind. It's rotting like my teeth," I said.

She gave one of her little warning coughs. "He's already saying that Jane has one of the finest minds in England."

"Why isn't she studying with Doctor Aylmer?"

"She will, when he returns from Leicestershire. Master Ascham's already started translating Virgil with her – *double* translation."

I scowled. Kat knew I would. Roger Ascham had promised to try out a new method of learning Greek: I was to translate from Greek into English. Then from my own English back into Greek, to make sure that it matched. It would be exacting. It would be exciting.

Ascham had already written a book about archery and he was going to write about education – *my* education.

"Ascham is *mine*, not hers," I grumbled. "Yes, bring my clothes, Kat. I'll go to lessons today. I won't be outshone by my little cousin."

But Roger Ascham was disappointed with me. He had given up the great minds of Cambridge to instruct a mind that had grown dull and dreary, a mind that if it sought the truth, must seek it in Bedlam.

Time after time, I stumbled over my words. I had once translated three pages of Virgil in an hour. My mind used to work with the speed of the sword. Now it hacked and chopped at the words.

Ascham winced. "I was told that you shone like a star," he said.

"The clouds came," I said, ungracious. "But I *am* thinking about something, although not about Virgil. How do we ever know the truth about anything or anybody?"

"Jesus said that He is the truth," Jane interrupted, "and the priests speak His truth."

I glared at her. "How can they?" I asked. "Priests said that there was Purgatory. Now they say there isn't. Priests said that the bread and wine changed into Christ's flesh and blood. Now they say it doesn't. Not even Archbishop Cranmer seems to know the truth, or want to tell it."

"Are you still unwell?" she asked.

"Yes, sick of your eyes bulging with piety."

I was sick of them both. I pleaded a headache and asked to leave.

"The Ancient Greeks used to apply electric eels to the head to cure melancholia," Ascham said, "until one madwoman snatched the eels from her head and ate them raw and writhing."

My stomach heaved.

I sat at my window. Dark clouds shadowed the sky beyond the river. A flash of lightning caught the lanterns of a barge. And a thought flashed into my mind with it, so simple and so wonderful that I laughed out loud. Unaccustomed to the sound these past weeks, Kat looked at me strangely and threatened to fetch me a calming cordial.

I am accustomed to the men around me having the power: Thomas Seymour, Edward Seymour, King Edward, my father, Robert Dudley, John Dudley... So accustomed to it that I had almost given away my power. In my childish innocence, I had waited for Francis to take me to his mother.

Why had I not thought it before? I did not need Francis.

I knew where Alys was. *I* would go to Bedlam.

If I went alone, I would be safe. If Alys refused to speak to me, I would have done my best. And if she did speak, I would lay my mother's ghost to rest.

I would go in springtime, when every leaf would hide me on the way to hell for I would have no Charon to row me.

I could wait.

Had my mother not waited six years for my father to marry her? Had I not already waited long enough to hear the truth?

The next morning, bright sunshine and birdsong told

me that the storm had passed. Into the darkness of February shone a few small suns: aconites, primroses and curling catkins.

The ice on the Thames cracked and water bubbled to the surface as sulphurous as hell. The river came back to life.

The sap was rising.

I ate like a horse. My stepmother pecked like her parrots. Her face was drained of colour. Her grey eyes were exhausted. I touched her burning forehead. "Are you unwell?" I asked, anxious.

"Yes. No." She laughed. "I am with child, Bess," she said. Her eyes brightened with happy tears. "It will be an autumn child like you and Edward and Jane, with red-gold hair and Tom's flashing green eyes…"

"It will be a boy?"

"Oh, yes, and Tom will be content at last."

We fell silent. Between us lay the ghosts of so many dead sons: Catherine of Aragon's and my mother's. Jane Seymour had borne a living son, but she had died from childbed fever. My belly twisted. I could not bear to be without Lady Catherine.

Impulsively, I took her hand and kissed it and in return, she kissed me on the cheek.

Kat's face darkened. When we were alone, she whispered, "When she's gone, you'll want me."

"But where's she going?" I asked, startled.

"A first child at thirty-six is foolish," she said. "But childbed or not, good people don't last long on earth. God always calls them to Him. I don't understand why. If he sent for the bad ones, we'd all sleep more safely in our beds."

When Kat went back to sleep in her own bedchamber, I knew that Thomas Seymour would be tempted by mine. I got up early, long before first light, and sat at the window seat. As my stepfather tiptoed in, I greeted him.

He pretended not to be startled. "This light isn't good enough to read by," he said. "That's why you're so short of sight."

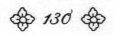

"I can see plain enough, sir."

He came to the window seat but I did not make room for him. "So what are you reading?" he asked.

"A poem," I said. "Thomas Wyatt wrote it for my mother."

"Poetry!" He sneered. "What a pity that Wyatt didn't lose his head along with the others. We wouldn't have to endure his lovesick lines now."

"Wyatt loved her long before my father but he didn't pursue her once my father fell in love with her. Listen. You'll like this: *There is written, her fair neck round about, Don't touch me* – Noli me tangere – *for Caesar's I am.*" I stared straight into his eyes. "*Noli me tangere,* sir."

He backed away. He never came to my bedchamber again.

Chapter Ten

"Edward and Anne Seymour have invited us to their new house on the Strand," Lady Catherine complained. "For Shrovetide," she added. She was pulling a face, but not in jest.

Shrovetide is one of our greatest feasts. It marks the beginning of the forty days of Lent, when we remember Christ's suffering before his crucifixion. Our earls and dukes and lords seek to outdo each other in their celebratory feasts.

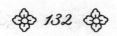

"I shall plead sickness and leave early," she said. "But you young ones must make merry after this long winter. There will be music again and dancing and all the other things we have missed."

"Will you come, Bess?" Jane asked.

"YES!" I cried. I thought of my mother, dancing like a butterfly blown by the breeze. "And I'll show the world that I'm better, that I've only been cocooned in my chrysalis this winter. And now the butterfly will emerge." I twirled around, as if she were still holding me. "I'll spread my wings this spring."

"Take care," Jane murmured. "Do not forget that butterfly wings are fragile."

The new house – Somerset House – was still unfinished. Wooden poles stretched from the roofs to the ground, as did last autumn's ivy, now grey with mould. But it would be splendid one day.

We were to dine and dance outside. Gardens, which would be glorious too, led down to the Thames. High tide and high wind together had allowed the river to seep into the lower garden, where it had frozen into a silver circle, like the moon beneath our feet.

Musicians strolled. Pigs roasted. Wine flowed faster than the water. Bundled in our furs against the bitter wind, we prowled like hungry wolves.

"Eat, drink and be merry, Bess," Thomas Seymour cried, "from tomorrow, forty days of fasting. No meat. No wine. No…" He winked at Robert Dudley and stopped himself. "It is as bad as the forty days' quarantine of the plague, though not as deadly. So, *carpe diem*, I say."

"And you say it badly, sir," Robert teased. "What will you give up for Lent, sweet Bess?"

"I've already given up what I love most," I said. "Sugar roses."

My stepfather roared with pleasure at my wit. He bore me no grudge. But I had not forgiven him. He must have already tainted me with tittle-tattle, if only in the kitchen.

Lute players struck the first chords of the galliard. My foot tapped. Nobody had danced in public since my father's death. Thomas Seymour bowed and led me onto

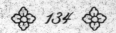

the ice. I was heavy in my sable fur, yet my feet were light. I did not feel the icy cold through my velvet shoes. My stepfather lifted me with ease, bringing me eye to eye with one of the lute players, a pretty boy who smiled at me.

The pleasure of the dance faded. Mark Smeaton had been a fine lute player at my mother's court. He had smiled at my mother and she had smiled back. He had been stretched on the rack until his young body broke, until he confessed that he had lain with her, and the next day watched his entrails taken from his twitching body. Some said that I was his child.

When my stepfather put me down, I froze. Seymour was impatient. He wanted to dance with the most beautiful girl in the garden – me. He wanted me to leap to the music. He wanted me to turn every head, both male and female…as my mother had done.

Puzzled, he asked, "Have you forgotten how to dance, Bess? You're as highly strung tonight as that lute."

"They think that I'm Smeaton's bastard," I whispered.

"Who?"

I was almost crying. "*Everybody.*"

 *135*

"The word belittles you, Bess." He released a curl from my headdress. "This is Tudor hair, down to the last strand. Smeaton's hair was as black as a moonless midnight. Nobody could doubt it. Do you think I'd care for you if it were otherwise?" He lifted me higher than before and people clapped at his daring. Then he handed me to Robert Dudley, who staggered with mock horror as he lifted me.

"I expected to find you thin and wasted," he said, "but you have…"

"…grown plump on sugar," I finished. "But I'm giving it up for Lent."

"And your mother, too, I hope." Robert tickled my back as he rushed me through the air. I shivered with excitement. Then he touched the nape of my neck briefly as he set me on the ground and I liked it as much as I had hated my stepfather's touch.

Robert and I stole into the Great Hall, although we had not yet been summoned inside. It too would be glorious by summer, when the walls had been panelled with wood and warmed with tapestries. For Shrovetide, the dais under the musician's gallery had been prepared for the evening's entertainment.

This dais was overhung with deep blue silk, painted with silver stars and a full moon. A veil of gossamer silk hung in front of a large table, which was draped with a golden cloth. Silver curtains hung at the sides of the dais. Along the bare walls of the hall, fire torches gave off a great heat and the perfume of lavender and thyme.

It was a sumptuous sight.

Outside, a trumpet fanfare summoned the other guests. Like ours, their winter-pale faces glowed at the sight. I made for the back of the hall, to stand closer to the door, but it was too late. The crowd of guests forced us to stay where we were. Thomas Seymour pushed his way to the side of the dais, pulling Jane behind him.

As soon as we were all assembled, an insistent drumbeat sounded from the gallery. Rising above it came the wail of a plucked viola string. A man's voice spoke from behind one of the silver curtains. "In a far-off desert lived King Herod, who had married his dead wife's sister, Herodias," he announced. "One of Jesus' disciples, John the Baptist, condemned Herod for what he had done…"

I gasped at the daring of it, for my father had married his dead brother's wife, Catherine of Aragon, and later blamed this marriage for his lack of a son. "Herod's wife had a beautiful daughter, Salomé, who danced better than any girl in the land…"

As his voice died away, fire torches were lit on the walls behind the veil, and a young woman began to dance barefoot on the table. Wrapped in silken cloths, she shimmered like the stars above us as she coiled and uncoiled to the rhythm of the drum, casting shadows across the veil that separated us.

Nobody could doubt the beauty of her curving body. Robert's wine dribbled from his lips and he circled his arm around my waist.

It was a clever ploy, for women are not permitted to dance for public display. I swayed with her, remembering how my mother had danced with me in her arms. If she had been here, would *she* have dared to dance for us? Would I have found the courage to dance with her?

The dancer was breathtaking. In seconds, Salomé had plucked us from the icy cold, carried us on her gossamer wings and set us down under the desert's starry sky. I forgot the past and the future. I only wanted to be her.

The music died. Salomé faded into the shadows as the fire torches were extinguished. "King Herod, moved by her great beauty, granted Salomé anything she wanted," the voice went on. "Salomé's mother whispered to her daughter, 'Ask for the head of John the Baptist on a silver platter. That will put an end to his evil talk about me.' And Salomé, a dutiful daughter, did as her mother commanded."

A trumpet blast brought an executioner onto the dais, sword in hand, eyes bulging through the holes in his black leather mask. Fear stabbed at me. "Whatever Lady Seymour has chosen to entertain us tonight, I want no part of it," I whispered to Robert. But he was still in his far-off desert and did not reply.

I could not push my way out. I closed my eyes instead. Only the sound of laughter that greeted John the Baptist made me look again. The veil had been drawn back. The table had been brought forward. In front of it stood a boy aged about ten or eleven, plump and pretty with golden hair as curly as a piglet's tail. His dark beard did not match his hair and this had provoked the laughter. I laughed a little too. After all, what had I to fear? This was only a Shrovetide spectacle.

Thomas Seymour stamped his foot, shouting, "Give us a man, not a boy. His beard droops like…" He whispered the next words and the men around him laughed. "Where did you get it? From John the Baptist's head?"

The terrified boy tried to run away, but the executioner caught him by the collar and pushed him up onto the table, where he lay face down.

A stench of mingled sweat and perfume caught the back of my throat. I wanted to retch. To a steady roll of the drum, the executioner raised his sword. At once, the mood changed from starry-eyed enchantment to barbarism, as softened lips bayed for blood. "Off with his head! Off with his head!" they shrieked.

Repelled, I wanted to look away. But I *had* to watch. The sword fell. Its blade thudded against the boy's neck,

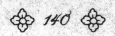

clouding his head with spurting blood, which splattered onto Jane. As it dispersed, I saw the gaping neck wound, ragged and bleeding.

This gruesome sight, and the stench of real blood that I recognized from the hunt, left me reeling. I had been spared the sight of my mother's death, but some in this hall must have witnessed it. Alys would have seen it. Jane was clutching her neck, gaping like a dead fish.

The severed head had appeared on the table at the feet of the headless corpse, its eyes rolling, its lips moving – and John the Baptist's beard swinging from side to side.

"I didn't know that Boleyn sprouted a beard in the Tower," a man shouted. "Perhaps she's not dead. Perhaps she paid a man to take her place."

Robert reached for my hand. I looked at them all: Tom Seymour doubled with laughter; Jane aghast at the blood on her neck; Anne Seymour sparkling at the success of her chosen entertainment. Even her husband was smiling.

Many feelings touched my tormented heart: anger, despair, humiliation. Powerful men had sent my mother to her death. Now powerful men mocked her memory.

Was this going to happen for the rest of my life, her memory reviled? No, I had listened in silence too long. I would not live like this any longer, my mother a shameful secret.

The real world pulled me back from my girlish dreams. I made my way to the dais, avoiding standing too close to the bloodied neck behind me. But curiosity got the better of me. A glance told me that the blood came from a circle of thick paste set around a hole in the table where the boy had hung his head. This paste had been impregnated with animal's blood. I ripped away the cloth to reveal his head below, and, further along, a second boy – his twin – poking his head through another hole.

"Spoilsport! Spoilsport!" The shouts deafened me.

"Get out of my sight before I roast you on the spit outside," I shouted. The boys dragged their bloodied heads from the holes and ran behind the curtain, giggling with fright.

Anne Seymour, upstaged, called me down, but I ignored her.

Only then did silence fall.

This is how it must have been for my mother on the scaffold, I thought. She gave a few well-chosen words in praise of my father before she went to her eternal silence. Did her heart almost stop beating, as mine seemed to now?

"As you can see, ladies and gentlemen, life is an illusion," I began. My voice shook. "We all see what we want to see, whether it is real or not. How I wish that my mother's death *had* been a trick. How I wish that she could have come alive like this piglet boy. She lies not far from here in an old arrow chest, because they forgot to order a coffin for her." I strengthened my voice. "I could not help her in her hour of need. I was only a baby. But I am a woman now..." A whistle cut the air and stopped abruptly. "...and one day *I* might be your Queen. So I command you not to speak of her in my presence, unless you have something good to say about her, because I shall *never* forget those who mock her tonight. If you do not know what to give up for Lent, then let it be mockery." I stopped, my heartbeat booming in my ears. Anne Seymour's newly-hung emeralds gleamed at me and gave me the courage to carry on.

"One day soon, I shall learn the truth about her and so shall you."

I finished, proud that I had defended my mother in public, proud that I had made my promise for all to hear. There was no lightning, no thunderbolt as I left the dais, only a rush of blood to my head. Some hissed. Some cheered. But all stood aside to let me pass. Some of the women curtsied. Some of the men bowed and doffed their caps. Thomas Seymour did neither. He stood, mouth gaping. It was the first time I had seen him lost for words.

Only Anne Seymour whispered as I passed, "We know the truth about your mother and you would do well to accept it quietly."

Promises made in public have even greater power than those made in private.

The truth, I thought. Now I *am* bound for Bedlam soon. There is no turning back.

Under the starlit sky, I removed the perfume box from my bodice, inhaling the faint fragrance that still

lingered there, for I had used up all the cream. I knelt. It was the first time I had done so outside the safety of my bedchamber – except in church. I never kneel in public, for I remember how my mother died. I would never give any swordsman the chance to steal up behind me and take off my head. "No more mockery, mother," I whispered. "Pray that Francis speaks the truth. Pray that Alys can tell me the truth."

Jane was the only one who came to comfort me, but she startled me badly, creeping up behind me. "He didn't really lose his head," she whispered. She rubbed her neck again and again. "Ellie says this is only bull's blood."

"You little fool!" I snapped. "Of course I know it isn't real. Don't you understand? They rubbed *my* face in the dirt of *my* past, in public, like you rub a puppy's nose in its own filth so that it will never foul in the same place again."

Her mouth trembled. "I would not dare make such a speech," she said. "My mother would beat me for it."

"Thank God that you have a mother," I shouted. "Better a cruel mother than a dead one."

Her thin shoulders heaved. She ran inside. I did not see her again that night. She left early with Mistress Ellen and Lady Catherine.

It was late when our barge returned for us. Guests still ate and drank, grasping the last moments before their fast. The sky was as black as ink, and extra lanterns had been lit on the barge. Thomas Seymour went to look for Kat, but he came back alone and told the oarsmen to start rowing. We left the water steps so quickly that I had no time to get out.

I shrank back into the shadows of the cushions and my furs. To be seen alone in a barge with a man – even my stepfather – would cause gossip.

In the bedchamber, I could run away or call for Kat. But in a barge, there was no escape, except into the murky Thames.

Seymour, silly with drink, shadowed me. When I moved away, he moved towards me. When I sat opposite him, he came to join me. "A performance as good as Salomé's," he said. He kissed my hand, eyes brimming

with open admiration, and placed his hand on my knee, beneath my furs. I pushed it away, repelled by him.

"I heard you scoff at my mother's death," I cried. "Did you know that your brother had chosen to insult her memory tonight?"

"Of course I didn't, Be— Elizabeth. I'm not so cruel – and neither is Edward. This illusion is the latest fashion in London, and Anne Seymour always seeks to be fashionable." His mouth was too close. "You're as beautiful as Salomé and you dance like her. So was your mother. I was a young man when she came to court. She bewitched with her black eyes..."

"Don't use that word."

"Oh Bess, she entranced, enthralled, enchanted, just as you did tonight."

I was not listening. I was thinking: on this royal barge of satin and silk was a man of great power, the Lord High Admiral of England, who protected everything except my reputation. Out there, in a boat that reeked of death was my half-brother, who had no power, whose mother was in Bedlam because of me.

Revulsion ran through me. "Remember your wife,

 147

sir, for she bears your child."

"Her lips aren't so inviting." He leaned over me, letting his beard brush my cheeks.

Would he never be finished with such talk? Would he always think I was like my mother? Full of pride that I had dared to defend her, I stood on tiptoe to reach him and, by the silly smile on his face, he thought I was trying to kiss him.

I tugged his beard and his eyes watered with pain. He cursed me. I cursed him. Then he lifted me off my feet, forcing me to let go. He dangled me in the air like a doll and I thought he would drop me into the Thames. Below, the icy water creaked against the sides of the barge and I thought of the girl in the death-boat, swollen with muddy water.

At last, my stepfather took pity on me, for my teeth clattered with cold. He threw me onto the cushions. Then he stood at the barge rail, cursing the oarsmen for their slowness, cursing all the way back to Chelsea.

Afraid, I cried into my gloves until the velvet was sodden. To calm myself, I watched the riverbanks flash by. Every candle had long been extinguished in the

little cottages. Leafless trees showed solitary walkers scurrying for the safety of their homes.

Such winter weeks had been the last weeks of my mother's life, although she had not known it. From the stillbirth of the son that would have saved her, till May Day, when she was taken to the Tower, she saw my father's affections change towards her. She could do nothing. She was a prisoner of vile gossip long before she was taken to be questioned.

I pondered. My mother went to the Tower on May Day, in full daylight for all to see her. Yet May Eve is a night of mystery and mischief, a night when anything can happen if you believe it can. It is a night for madness.

It was the night I would go to Bedlam.

I snuggled deep into my sable furs and thanked God that I had made up my mind. At last, I dared hope. If Francis had told me the truth, I might speak to somebody who had loved my mother. I might unburden myself of the thoughts and doubts that had obsessed me for so long.

❖ ❖ ❖

Servants were waiting at the water steps with flaming torches that would guide us back to Chelsea Palace.

"I'll wait for Kat," I said.

Seymour scowled. "Don't wait too long. People will talk."

I stood in the warmth of the fire braziers, watching their flickering glow on the water, warming my cheeks. On these steps, I had first seen Francis. On these steps my mother had come back to haunt me. Soon I would lay her ghost to rest.

Kat came in on the Dudley's barge. She was snoring as it moored. As soon as she saw me, she grumbled at me, her voice thick with sleep. "You shouldn't have been alone with *him*."

"He tricked me, Kat," I said. "But I won't let him trick me again – ever."

We set off for the house, arm in arm. Above us, rose stalks entwined, their thorns sparkling in the frost like tiny swords.

Yes, it was decided. I would go on May Eve, when anything can happen. And pray to God that I would hear the truth.

Chapter Eleven

How can you sleep when you know you have to go to hell?

Night after night, I watched the river, whipped to waves by March gales and flattened by damp mists.

I wished the days away.

The first blossom – hawthorn, bright against its black branches – set my heart racing. Then nature moved with the speed of the spring tides. Every day, leaves thickened on the trees, buds swelled, bees sucked.

I commanded time to stop. But it rolled on, as relentless as the river.

On May Eve, the kitchens gave off the scent of pies and puddings and sweet pastries. Maggie scolded the maids Mary and Bess for sitting on the kitchen steps, weaving marsh marigolds into a garland for the kitchen door. Tonight, they would bring back may blossom to garland the doors and gates.

I was ready. Over the past few days, whenever Kat had gone to gossip with Mistress Ellen, I had picked lavender for my pomander. I had placed my black velvet shoes and cloak under my bed. I did not fear Kat knowing what I would do. She hated May Eve for the noisy merrymaking that kept her from her sleep and she had already prepared her poppy-flower cordial.

But the path to truth is fraught with danger. I feared Bedlam as much as I had feared hell when I was a child, peeping into my father's kitchen.

What if the devil swallowed me and did not spit me out? *Who* would know? *Who* would rescue me?

Robert Dudley was the only person who knew about Francis. I would trust him with my deadliest of secrets.

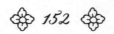 152

❖ ❖ ❖

Picnics were Lady Catherine's greatest pleasure. On the afternoon of May Eve, all that could be carried was brought from the house to the rose arbour: tables, benches, cushions, all set upon a richly patterned carpet. The arbour formed our walls, the rosebuds our ceiling. The parrot cages were hung from the wooden posts. Excited by the new scents, they fluffed out their bright feathers and snapped the air for insects who had dared to enter their cages. Sometimes they stretched out their beaks to peck the rose petals, and I could not bear it.

We all dreamed in the warming sun – my stepmother of the son she might bear; Jane of God, no doubt; and Kat and Mistress Ellen of their past a-Mayings before they became too noisy.

I dreamed of my new self. Would I look any different in the morning? As my eyes shone with the truth, would people whisper, "What a beautiful young woman our Princess Elizabeth is. She has left childhood behind."

But first, to hell – and back.

❖ ❖ ❖

I invited Robert Dudley to walk with me down to the river.

Kat straightened my headdress, smoothed my dress as if I were a bride. It was no more than tomfoolery, we knew that, because a royal marriage is decided by men of the Privy Council. But this was done with merriment, in honour of May. "In Spring, a young woman's fancy turns to love," she said.

"A rosebud is too young for love," Mistress Ellen said.

"Will you beg him to go a-Maying with you tonight?" Jane asked.

"Princesses don't go a-Maying." I gave a laugh, halfway between despair and terror.

They looked from one to the other, as if the sun had already boiled my brain.

"I've told you again and again, don't laugh like that," Kat warned. "You sound just like your mother."

"And what's wrong with that?" I asked.

Robert and I walked under the roses. I felt my mother's presence in the unfolding rosebuds. Tonight, I would

meet somebody who had loved her, and I would ask all the questions that had lain in my mind all my life, ever since I could remember. And, God willing, I would hear the truth.

Kat followed at a distance, giggling like a girl when Robert took my arm. Neither of us had mentioned Francis again, but his presence was unseen between us. I could smell him.

"Robert?"

He stopped, recognizing the begging tone in my voice. "If it's about that boy again, Bess, the answer's still NO."

I stood on tiptoe to smell the roses. "I'm not *asking* today, Robert. I'm telling. It's something Kat doesn't know and she mustn't know – *ever*. Sometimes she lets the truth spill after a glass of wine. I spoke to Francis… the boy in the boat…at Twelfth Night."

His face darkened. "You've spoken to *that* creature? Oh, Bess, *why?*"

"You know why. I'm going to see his mother tonight."

"She'll cut off a lock of your hair and mix it with bat's droppings or rat's p—" He kicked a wooden post,

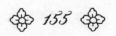

making a parrot cage swing. The other parrots set up an ear-splitting squawk. "It smacks of witchery and worse."

"You're the only person I really trust, Robert. Do you remember, on my birthday, you promised to be my eyes? Well, look for me tomorrow at the joust. If I'm not there, will you come and find me?"

"Let me come with you."

I shook my head. "No. It would be too dangerous to be seen together. And I don't trust Thomas Seymour. He knows that we're close in our affections. He might use it against you one day."

"Then don't involve me at all," he said.

"I must, Robert, for I'm going to the worst place on earth."

Robert cursed. "Where?" he asked.

Kat came closer.

I whispered "Bedlam", as Francis had done. Robert drew out his sword and hacked at the rose heads. He was close to tears. "Let me rid you of Francis," he said.

"I know what you're thinking. But Alys isn't mad, Robert. She isn't… Although if this *is* a plot to be rid

of me… Well, it will be too late to find me anyway. I'll probably be at the bottom of the Thames."

"He's dangerous, Bess. You'll never be safe as long as he's here. That's what men like him do. They go for the weakest—"

"I'm not weak."

"You're a woman. He tells you a pitiful tale and you believe him. He's used you. Let me protect you. That's what men are for." As we reached the river, he pleaded with me again. "How can I stop you, Bess?"

"You can't."

"You're a fool to go," he said.

"And I'd be a fool not to," I replied.

But my words sounded hollow as I stood by the sunlit river with Robert. I wished that I did not have to go to Bedlam. I wished that I could forget the past.

Robert bowed and kissed my hand. Then he leaned over to kiss me. I waited, my skin tingling. But then Kat was between us, pushing us apart.

Strange, I thought. She had not truly protected me from Thomas Seymour.

With a short bow to Kat, Robert went straight to

 157

his barge. "I've lost my taste for picnics," he said.

"What have you said to ruffle his feathers?" Kat asked.

"Nothing – except the truth. And now he hates me for it."

"No, he doesn't," Kat said. "Hate and love are opposite sides of the same coin, that's all. It just depends which way it falls. Hate today. Love tomorrow."

Tomorrow. If I had known what was to happen before dawn, I would have never left my bed.

Chapter Twelve

I came face-to-face with Maggie in the kitchen, although it was long past dusk. Smooth-cheeked and smooth-lipped, she stumbled with her swift curtsy in her eagerness to meet her sweetheart.

"Maggie, wrap some rose petals for me," I said. There was disapproval on her face as she took in my black velvet cloak and hidden hair. "May not a princess go a-Maying?" I asked.

"Yes, but not alone, Your Grace."

"Mistress Ashley dislikes May Eve."

"Folks'll talk. They'll say 'tis only witches that go out alone in the dead o' night." It was an innocent remark or a well-intentioned warning as it turned out, but with nerves already taut, I slapped her. Her cheek, so carefully whitened, flushed. She took a spoonful of salt and twisted it into a piece of muslin. "Best sprinkle this as you go then," she said, "lest the devil comes for you."

Anger fuelled me through the gardens and to the woods. I ran so fast that sweethearts parted to let me pass.

I forgot Maggie. I forgot the men of the old faith.

The woods were intoxicating to a princess never allowed out alone at night. The air, scented with may blossom and rambling roses, bluebells and foxgloves, spoke of laughter and love. Evil could not linger here.

Moonlight had worked its magic, lighting up the trees to create a fairyland, making darker hollows where young men and women kissed. All the young women I met were dressed in white, glowing like fairies out to make mischief. Around me, birds, confused by the brightness and noise, sang their hearts out.

What would it be like to go a-Maying with Robert Dudley, to laugh and love alone with him away from prying eyes? We could run barefoot, picking may blossom, unwatched except by other lovers, equally under love's spell and we would gaze, enchanted, into each other's eyes until dawn.

But Maggie was right. The sight of a black-cloaked woman alone at night made the young men draw their sweethearts close and call out "witch", and I envied the girls to be cosseted and caressed.

At the edge of the woods, I turned towards the river path. I remembered it well from my riding. It narrowed and darkened under twining trees. Little moonlight penetrated the trees here and I felt my way as if I had no sight. Brambles caught my cloak, tugging me back and I had to pull hard to free myself, spoiling the soft cloth. I could have been playing blind man's bluff.

But those childish days were done.

I was alone.

Here and there, a glimmer of moonlight on evening dew showed the way, and so too did the lanterns of barges so heavily garlanded that the woods seemed to

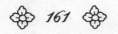

have taken to the water. One of the boatmen offered me a ride free of charge for the beauty that he knew must be hidden by my hood, but I ignored his calls. It was not a risk I would take.

I walked under the trailing willows, exhausted not by the walk, but by the fear of what was to come. Branches creaked. Twigs snapped. I remembered the men in the woods.

About a mile further on, the sweet scented air of Chelsea gave way to the stench of London. My cloak was already ripped, my shoes near ruin, my breathing uneven. I stopped to catch my breath. A terrible thought came to me. What if Francis had already taken his mother back to France? Why should she wait for me?

I slowed, almost blinded by tears.

In my heart, I was afraid, although I did not want to admit it. Soon, I would have to pass the water steps of Whitehall Palace, and the Seymour and Dudley houses. I would have to take my chance, darting from shadow to shadow past the guarded water steps or worse, brave the streets of London.

Between the devil and the deep sea.

 162

❖ ❖ ❖

At Westminster, before I came to Whitehall, I decided to risk the streets rather than the river path. Reluctantly, I turned away from the water with its cooling midnight mists; from the silver thread that would take me to Alys.

I plunged into a narrow street. I had never walked in a street before. In palaces, people move with purpose and good manners. They part as I pass. Not here. I pushed and elbowed my way between beggars, drunkards and cutpurses. This was May Eve – a wild night of no curfew – when anything might happen.

The street brought me to the great hunting park behind my brother's palace, teeming with May merrymakers and disgruntled deer running away to hide.

It is not possible to be lost in London. Its churches and towers and turrets are its landmarks. Now the steeple of St Paul's Church beckoned. The streets that took me there were the worst: stinking of rotting vegetables and animal hides; of dung from stables and pigs and horses; of the sick who lived there.

Even the dead stank. The churchyard at St Paul's gave off a cloying stench of rotting corpses.

I did not expect to find hell outside Bedlam.

So this was the life that lay beneath the silver and gold and glitter of my life. Like the mud that oozed below the sparkling river, I had known that it was there. Had I not glimpsed it on my birthday? But now I saw it in all its awfulness, so putrid that no blossom, no may greenery could disguise it.

I shuddered and thanked God that I had been born to the King and Queen of England.

I feared it all. It would take only one bolder than the rest to pull back my hood, to recognize me and call out my name. What then? Would they eat from my hand or stab me in the back?

With my last strength and courage, I made my way north to Bishops Gate. Beyond the gate, two open drains carried filth away from a building that had the look of a monastery – a sloping roof of cloisters on two sides, a bell tower, an arched doorway. It was situated in the foulest place that God could have created and I wondered if he had not delegated its creation to the devil.

A silver coin gave me entry to Bedlam. Another bought me light – yet no lantern, only a candle slender enough to remind me that I should not linger there. The guard drew back the creaking bolt on the door. A vile stench rose to meet me. I hesitated, glancing beyond the city wall to Moor Field, as if taking my last view of the world. Moonlight caught the sails of a windmill and the steeple of a little church. Cloths stretched out to dry and, whatever their colour, the moonlight had touched them all with silver.

The guard waited. He looked past me, as if he had seen women like me many times.

They say that my mother hesitated only once when she arrived at the Tower. She sank to her knees on the steps and wept. Then she went inside.

The door of Bedlam gaped. I filled my lungs with air and stepped into the mouth of the devil himself. I did not expect to come out alive.

Chapter Thirteen

We each have our own idea of hell. Priests preach of roasting on an everlasting fire. Artists paint the devil shouting from gaping mouths. When I was a child, it had been my father's fiery kitchen.

I saw no fire in Bedlam. There was no such comfort. But I saw the devil. He was everywhere, in swollen lips that blasphemed and cursed, in twisted bodies naked for all to see, in fingers smearing walls with their own filth.

For them, no warm caresses.

I thought that I had been to Bedlam in my mind when I had been ill during the dark days of winter. But I had not smelled it. Its stench was worse than the river mud, for it stank of human filth. Water – or worse – pooled on the flagstones. I recognized the odour at once. It was the rank smell of Francis.

God had left this place. In the cloisters, where monks had once walked in quiet moonlit contemplation, men and women screeched in torment, stretching their chains to the limits to touch me. Nobody slept. How could they in the deafening roar of their companions' cries, each lost in their own witless world?

"Alys?" I called. Nobody answered.

I ran through the cloisters, repeating her name. Then I turned into a windowless corridor of dank walls patterned with darting insects, as foul-smelling as the cloisters I had left behind. My ruined shoes squelched on flagstones thick with slime.

Just when I thought that I would have to run back to the door and beg to be let out, a glorious smell came to me: rosemary, mint and may blossom. From a doorway came dim candlelight and the sound of clicking, like the parrots when they snapped insects.

I looked in.

A candle stub lit a small cell, casting its shadow over a woman sitting on the flagstones. They were strewn with the herbs and blossom I had smelled. She was knitting with four wooden needles that formed a circle. I remembered Francis's strange hat.

For a second, I thought, *Is* she my mother? Were those who had jeered at Shrovetide right? Had they pretended to chop off her head and kept her alive to bring her back to me?

A silly fancy, and so it was.

As she leaned over the needles, I saw that her scalp was scabby, like Francis's forehead. Her hair was wispy and white, except for a single strand of black which was as glorious as my mother's. Her clothes I could scarcely see, except that they held together in their filthy greyness.

I stepped towards her. "Alys?" I asked. I pushed back my hood and shook out my hair.

She looked up, wept a little. "You were only two

years old when I last saw you, when your mother brought you to Greenwich," she whispered. "She could not stop kissing you that day." The chain did not allow her to stand upright, but pulled her into a curtsy by chance. "Francis said you would have the courage to come alone."

At last I looked at the face of my father's mistress.

In my mind, I had imagined her to be as old as my mother would have been – almost fifty. But Alys was little more than thirty, in spite of the way she looked. Francis was right. She was no great beauty. Her nose was too big, her chin too small; but her skin looked as soft as silk. She must have only been my age when she had served my father. I stared a full minute, not at her face and hair, but into her eyes. They were not the eyes of a madwoman. They were as clear and as bright as my mother's emeralds.

My voice was sharper than I had intended, for I fought to control my tears. I could not let my heart soften, not just yet. "Madam, how do I know that you mean me no harm? I have risked my reputation – and perhaps my life – by coming to you alone and at night.

Will you swear on your Bible that you will speak the truth?"

She stiffened. "Do you see a Bible in this godforsaken place? No, it has long since been stolen. And how do I know that you've not come to harm me? Why isn't Francis with you? How do I know that he hasn't already been taken to the Tower, accused of treason?" Alys resumed her knitting, cursing as she dropped a stitch. "Oh, yes, you're certainly your mother's daughter," she mumbled. "Outspoken and haughty and sure of her place in the world. As you can see, I know my place, chained to a wall."

I begged her forgiveness. At last, she relented and put down her knitting. "Your mother used to bring apples and pears and bread for the lost souls of Bedlam. But that was long before I knew her."

I blushed. I had forgotten to bring the rose petals. I had only salt in my pocket.

"She came *here*?"

"Yes. Her brother George was Governor of Bedlam, before she was Queen."

Now I understood my feverish winter dream – my

mother laughing and holding the hand of a young man with eyes as dark as hers, handing out food to bony fingers poking through bars.

I knelt before Alys so that she could sit in comfort. "Alys, I'm sorry that you're here because of me."

"No, it's because of my father," she replied. "It's the fate of most of the women here. It bothers me less than I expected now that I've given up the freedom of my life in France. In fact, I've grown used to my little chamber away from the cruel world."

I took her hand. "Why did my mother sign a marriage annulment?" I asked. "Why did she take away my royal name? Did she fear the flames? Did she hate the thought of men seeing her body when her clothes had melted away?"

Alys sighed. "She did it for her brother. He was to be hung, drawn and quartered and then burned. He would have watched his own entrails burn outside his body and she couldn't bear the thought. By agreeing to annul her marriage, his sentence was changed to beheading. She loved her brother as...I hope you might love yours."

"Is that what you really want from me?" I asked. "Your son's birthright?"

"No, and neither does he."

The questions tumbled from me like the water that had gushed from the drowned girl's mouth. "Alys, was my mother guilty of adultery?"

"No. *Never*. The charges were made up to be rid of her. Catherine of Aragon was the thorn in your father's flesh for many years. He did not want the same to happen when he married Jane Seymour. This time, he wanted your mother dead, not divorced. Everybody knew the charges were false. At her trial they read out the dates of her adultery. I was with your mother every day and night, child. On every supposed date, she was with child, or recovering from childbed or the birth of a dead son."

As I listened, my mother rose from her dust and darkness. The lies, the accusations, the slander all dispersed.

"Was she a…" I did not want to say the word. "Was she ever…a witch? Did my mother ever curse Catherine of Aragon and cause her death?"

"*Never*. It was all cruel tittle-tattle. She cursed only herself for not bearing a live son." She looked at me with pride. "You are so like her...she had a temper as sharp as a snake's tongue, as I believe is yours, so Francis tells me...but she needed it. She had so many enemies at court. Thomas Cromwell was the worst...but she was a good match for him."

It was like being bathed in my mother's perfume. I closed my eyes and let it seep into my hair and skin. I let it soak every speck of mud from me.

At last I was truly cleansed.

I laughed. All my life I had laughed to please, to flatter, to hide my fear. Now I laughed for joy.

"Thank you from the bottom of my heart for my mother's perfume," I said. "Now I have seen her as I did when I was a child. Tell me something I never saw. What was she like with my father? What was she like at court?"

Alys understood my rapture. Her voice danced. "Oh, where shall I begin? She was such fun. She danced and sang and talked of everything, and she enchanted men and women. It's true that she used all her female charms

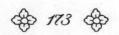

and wiles on your father. But they loved each other with such passion." As Alys brought my mother to life, her face softened with her memories. Her back straightened. Her voice steadied. She showed the pride she had felt to have been the Gentlewoman of the Queen of England. "But when she miscarried the child…your brother…she felt her power wane and…"

"She became shrill and demanding," I said. "That's what I'm like when I'm afraid."

Sometimes, screams pierced our conversation. They froze my blood, but Alys did not turn a hair. "She was as tempestuous as an end-of-summer storm. The storms would have given way to blue sky if his sons had lived. She almost died by miscarrying her last son. There was hardly any blood left to spill."

My head swam, threatening to send me sprawling onto the straw. I swayed, felt my own blood drain away. The walls pressed against my chest, taking away my breath. I began to pant.

"Gently, child. Let out your breath slowly and you'll fight your fear. Your mother would have been a great Queen if she had lived, and so will you if…you do nothing

 174

that can give cause for tittle-tattle," she finished.

She picked up her knitting, lost in her own thoughts and I knew that it was time to leave. I did not want to go back into the hell outside. I wanted to stay with Alys. It was like being with my mother in my memories. I felt safe with her.

I forced myself up, kissed her hand and went to the door. But as I reached the door, she said, "Elizabeth, Your Grace, your parents' life together was like a play, acted for all to see, and like the best plays it was full of tears and laughter, revenge and love…and death always waiting in the wings. Don't forget, sweet child, that you will *never* be the only player on the stage. And don't pity me. I've grown quite fond of my little cell. I feel safe." She held up her candle and laughed. "I have shadows for company. I can talk about your mother as much as I want and nobody believes me."

I ran back to her, sank beside her and embraced her.

Beyond Bedlam, I breathed deeply before I plunged back into the stinking streets. But breathe deeply I did,

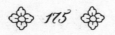

for I was full of joy. It was not just the truth that had released me. It was the pleasure of talking about my mother that made my feet light.

I did not realize they had come for *me*, the young girls who fluttered from the side streets, white and scarlet and frilled, like butterflies. They held me firmly by the arm. I could not shake them off. "Who are you? Where are you taking me?" I cried.

But my new ladies-in-waiting escorted me in silence. "I command you to answer me." I kicked out at the nearest girl, but she sidestepped me, as if she had been kicked too many times in her life.

We came to London Bridge, where the water churns between its arches. Then I was more afraid than I had been, even in Bedlam. I dared not scream. I did not want to give myself away.

There the river roared in my ears. I thought of the young girl in Francis's boat, the arch of her swollen body, torrents of muddy water gushing from her mouth.

I closed my eyes to take away the horror.

If I died now, I would die knowing the truth about

my mother. I would face death as bravely as she had. And another thought came: I would die without ever being kissed by a man, and that was the saddest thought of all.

"So you've caught in a live one at last," one of the girls said, and she giggled; but there was no malice in her voice.

A man thanked them and sent them on their way – a man who smelled of decay and death, a man who was used to speaking French. I opened my eyes.

Francis stood in his rotten boat. "Don't despise them," he called. "We all sell bodies."

"You're everywhere, like the plague," I called back. "Did you send them for me?"

"Yes."

"How did you know I was there?"

"I saw you as I was leaving," he replied. "I visit my mother every day."

"But how did you know it was me?"

He smiled. "You walk like a Queen."

"That's because my mother was one." I glared at him. "Have you come to kill me? Then I'll be one person less

between you and the throne. How? Ah – yes. It will be the river. That's what you know best. Then you'll pick up my body and earn four pence. Rich pickings for a princess, didn't you say?" I laughed, half from terror, half despair. "Perhaps you're plotting with Mary. Are you of the old faith? Most people in France are."

He sighed. "Faith is of little importance to me." He jumped from his boat and I fingered my little dagger in my pocket.

Francis must have seen the fear on my face because he used my name for the first time. "Your Grace, Princess Elizabeth…you've had the courage to enter hell tonight. You've faced the devil. Now you'll have the courage to face the rest of your life, for nothing will ever be as bad. I speak as one who knows."

"You're as silver-tongued as my father," I said.

"I've had you brought here so that I can take you safely home to Chelsea," he said.

"Swear to me that this isn't a plot to kill me," I insisted. I searched in my mind for something to help make this safe. "Zeus used to bring his gods to hell's river to swear their sacred oaths. If they lied, he made them drink its

poisoned water and it paralysed them. Swear on this great river that—"

"You're not in your snug schoolroom now," Francis replied, angry. "*My* world's raw and cold and dangerous. So I'll speak plainly. I don't lie and you don't need to threaten me with stupid tales of poisoned water and gods that never existed." He got up and walked back to his boat. "Do you want me to take you or not?" In spite of his anger, there was suddenly a gentle pleading in his voice.

Still I hesitated. "My mother made her last journey along this river on May Eve – the royal barge was her death-boat. How do I know that your death-boat will not be mine?"

"You don't," he snapped.

Still I did not put my dainty shoe into the boat and he became impatient. "It will cost me dear if I don't work tonight." He untied the rope and picked up his oars.

I once asked Kat how we knew that God existed. *Well, we don't*, she said. *We have to make a leap of faith.*

I made my leap of faith – into a boat so rank and rotten that even the branches of may blossom scattered

179

inside could not disguise the stench of death.

"How can your mother bear Bedlam?" I asked.

"She promised your mother to give you her perfume and to tell you the truth if she could," he replied. "A promise is a promise. She would have died for love of your mother. She would die for you. That's what love is."

It was a mystery to me. If loving somebody meant dying for them, would love be for me?

We did not speak again until we reached Whitehall Palace. There, Francis let the boat drift. At the spot where we had seen the drowned girl, my nerves were stretched to breaking. All my fear returned. Francis could tip me into the water whenever he chose.

His lantern cast shadows across his face. His beard, like Robert Dudley's, was beginning to thicken, giving him a greater likeness to the portrait of my father. "I don't want to be part of this...your life," he said. "It stinks, like me. Why do men fight for every scrap of power? Why do they fight over God? It's the same in France, now that King François is dead. Here Catholics hide in the woods to pray. There Protestants hide in

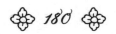

castles with walls so high that only the birds can hear their prayers. One day, there'll be terrible slaughter between the two. I'll not stay in France once I've taken my mother back. There are other lands…"

"The New World?" I asked.

"No, further north…lands so vast that it doesn't matter who I am, lands so cold that ships are stuck in the ice all winter, lands with forests full of bears…"

"Aren't they as dangerous as the Dudleys and the Seymours?" I asked.

He laughed. "Yes. But their fur will keep me warm in winter."

Towards Chelsea, dawn rose, casting pearls of shimmering light along the water. Francis rowed into the riverbank between Chelsea Village and the palace. I did not want to part from him and I begged him to stay for a while. The boat rocked gently in the wash of passing barges, swinging the lantern.

"Thank you, Francis for what you've done," I said. "I'm sorry that I didn't trust you, but a dozen boys a day claim to be my father's son and…"

"The stench of death doesn't invite trust," he replied.

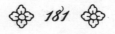

"I could bring you some camomile," I said.

"What for?"

"For your sores," I said.

"We can't meet again. Tonight we're safe. Nobody believes what happens on May Eve. But any other night…"

"It's been the happiest night of my life," I whispered. "But you can't leave your mother in Bedlam any longer, Francis. I won't let you." I fumbled inside my pockets and pulled out all the coins left – a good sum. "You've been a faithful ferryman tonight. Accept your payment. Take your mother back to France now."

He swallowed hard, as if he had never seen such gold and silver. "If I was found with money, I'd be accused of theft, bribery, conspiracy. No, it's too dangerous. I'll earn our passage."

"But that will take for ever. You cannot leave her there."

He shrugged.

Suddenly I was exhausted. I wanted to wash off the stench of Bedlam. I wanted to be back in my warm bed at Chelsea Palace. Francis sensed it. He held onto a branch to steady his boat and helped me out. I put out my hand for him to kiss. "Think of me," he said. "I'll be in some far-off land, but king in my own way."

"Farewell, Francis. And until you leave London, be on your guard, although the danger will not come from me."

"And you too, My Lady Elizabeth," he replied. "Keep your back against the wall, like my mother."

I watched him row away, bowed with the strain.

Tears welled. "Francis, one day, when I have the power...if ever I am Queen...I'll recognize who you are." But he did not hear me, for I had whispered the words, and he had already disappeared into the lapping darkness.

I walked slowly at first, tearful. Then my spirits rose and I ran, not from fear this time, but from delight. I skimmed the ground like a bird. The moon was sinking in a sky dark-blue with dawn; the river horizon already glowed with daylight.

My mother was no witch, I wanted to shout. And I

am no witch's daughter. She was no adulteress. I am no adulteress's daughter.

Words can only hurt if you fear some truth in them. When they have not, they lose their power. So when an old man called out, "Witch," I called back, "Not me, sir, nor my mother." And hearing the lightness in my voice, he let me be.

I threw off my hood. I picked may blossom to garland my hair and danced my way back. I was Queen of the May, Queen of the enchanted woods that night, the maidens I met no more than fairies at my feet, their sweethearts no more than elfin creatures. And one day, if I wore the crown of England, I would be the greatest Queen England had ever known.

If only my happiness had not gone to my head that night, I might still be safe at Chelsea Palace. But I let it spill out for all to see and turned it into misery before the night was done. The enchantment was broken.

There was nobody to save me that perfect May dawn.

Chapter Fourteen

In the gloom of the kitchen, I thought it was Maggie hunched over the fire, turning over the last glowing embers in the hearth, until the figure turned and asked, "Where have you been, Bess?" The scent of sugar wafted from the pastry kitchen beyond.

It was my stepfather.

Startled that it was him, I stammered, "H-h-how did you know that I…?"

His lips were sulky. *"Only witches go out at night alone."*

He mimicked Maggie's voice. "I've trained Maggie well, Bess, and not just how to make your roses. She knows how to please me, that's why I brought her from Gloucestershire. But she liked you. If you hadn't slapped her, she might not have come to tittle-tattle to me tonight." He got up, staring at me in the faint light from the window. He took in the burrs and bramble leaves clinging to my cloak, my torn girdle, the garland in my tangled hair. "You look different, Bess. What have you been up to, my little princess? Where have you been? A-Maying with sweet Robert Dudley?"

"Just a-Maying." I stayed by the door, ready to run. But he came close, took the garland from my head and threw it into the dying coals, where it sizzled, scenting the kitchen. Then he sniffed my face and hair, his beard tickling my neck as it had done that first morning. "You stink, Bess. You reek of evil. Have you been riding with the devil tonight? Are you still innocent?"

Oh, why did I answer him? Why did I not make my way straight to my bedchamber? And why did I tell the truth?

I pushed his face away. "Not so innocent, sir, though

not in the way that you mean," I replied. "The devil has more shapes and sounds than I could ever have imagined and I've seen them all tonight. Sir, I've been to hell and back."

He did not understand, and he did not ask. But he noticed that the happiness drained from me as I recalled the lost souls in Bedlam. "So what's made you so happy and so sad? Only a man could do that..." His eyes flashed, jealous.

"You're wrong, sir," I cut in. "It's a woman who has made me so, by telling me how my innocent mother was brought to her death so that my father could marry your sister..."

"And where did you learn this great truth, Bess?"

"In..." I stopped. "She helped my mother in her darkest times...one of her own ladies-in-waiting...but in doing so, she brought about her own ruin by bearing my father's son."

Thomas Seymour's face did not darken with anger or surprise. He whistled under his breath. Then he laughed, quietly at first, then loud enough to wake the dead. He laughed until spittle trickled through his beard and

dripped from the last curled hair onto the flagstones. "So he was another pup mewling for its master."

I leaned against the table, exhausted and appalled that I had said so much. "This pup's as much my brother as Edward."

"Though not born to a Queen," he said.

I was hot, even though the fire had almost died. The stench of Bedlam overwhelmed me. I wanted to wash.

"You've been unwise, Bess. You must let *me* teach you. That's what I'm here for. Ascham can teach you how men used to live...Horace and Virgil...and...I forget the others, but they were men who lived by the pen. Forget them, Bess. In this new world, men must live by the sword."

"Or die by it."

"May Eve turns minds to love, but also to hate," he whispered. "What if this woman hates your mother for spoiling her life and she's taking her revenge by feeding you lies?"

He could not hurt me any more with his cunning. "I trust her," I said. "And if you cared for me, you'd be happy for me."

"I *do* care, and that's why I'm afraid for you, Bess. The pup and his bitch mother have used you badly. What if they're plotting the King's downfall? How will this look to the Privy Council? You've put us all in danger, you little fool. It smacks of treason."

Treason. The word that chills the heart.

Exhausted. Excited. Now afraid. I was no longer sure of anything. And Thomas Seymour saw it.

"His mother has bewitched you, Bess," he whispered. "Like your mother bewitched." I was truly exhausted, but I would not cry. I knew his cunning now: mention my mother so that I would cry and he could comfort me. "Do you remember what I told you at Shrovetide? She rubbed love potions onto her lips to attract a man as honey attracts a bee…as your lips attract me now." He pulled my lips together to turn them into a smile. His beard tickled my face again. Then he leaned over and kissed me full on the lips as a man kisses a woman, suffocating me, repelling me with his early morning breath.

The kiss of Judas.

Revulsion. Rage. Shame. All three – but mostly shame. I did not tug his beard. I remembered his dangerous strength from Shrovetide. I endured it.

Can you find such potions to make you hate, that I can put on my lips – or his?

O Dieu, m'aidez! Oh God, help me.

Only a pitiful moan made him let go. It came from Lady Catherine. I saw her over his shoulder, standing in the soft light, eyes and hair wild, clutching her swollen belly as if to protect her unborn child from the sights and sounds of her husband's folly. I continued to stare at her, my face smarting from the scratch of his beard.

"Traitors!" she called out.

Yes, the worst word. But how could she think otherwise? Me, alone with her husband as dawn broke, both dressed as if we had just returned from some secret assignation. It would have been better if we had been wearing our nightclothes, as if we had chanced upon each other on a sleepless May Eve, when the rest of the world was out a-Maying.

"You fool, Tom," she said. "To kiss the King's sister is treason. I know that you're a vain and arrogant man, but I longed for a healthy body in my bed after six years of a King who wanted only a nurse in his." She fixed me with her wild eyes. "And you're an even greater fool, Bess. I welcomed you as my own daughter, begging your father to give you back your name, to welcome you to court, and this is how you repay me. Like mother, like daughter?"

I winced. I had never known Lady Catherine to be cruel. "I've done nothing wrong," I said.

"Look at you, child, flushed from first kissing. I wanted you to live with me for ever so that I could take the place of your misguided mother who bewitched every man she met. I *warned* you, Bess. You've crossed the line now – the invisible line, and who knows if you'll ever make it back to the other side."

"But I've learned the truth about my mother tonight. She *was* innocent. That's what I've been telling T…your husband."

"I did not hear you speak, Elizabeth. I only saw you kiss."

Then she was gone.

Thomas Seymour did not follow his wife, but went into the garden. The open door let in shafts of sunlight, and the perfumes of a perfect May Day.

 *191*

I went into the pastry kitchen, pulled the muslin cloth from the silver tray, scattering flies. On the tray lay a sugar rose, every petal clean and curled.

Maggie's best rose yet.

You will grow into the most beautiful rose England has ever known, my mother had said.

My beauty now blemished. I crammed the rose into my mouth, worked my tongue around its petals until it dissolved. Its sweetness overwhelmed me.

But it was not enough. I returned to the kitchen, gorged on the rose petals drying on the window sill until my stomach heaved. I tipped the remaining trays onto the floor and stamped on the crisped petals. They released a heavenly fragrance and clouds of sugar, settling on my hair like may blossom. My shoes were sticky with sugar, my eyelashes and hair clogged with them, until Kat was slapping my cheeks, shaking me, and I clung to her, crying, "Oh, Kat, why did I go out tonight?"

Morning streamed through the window. Birdsong began. A perfect May Day, shattered into a thousand pieces. Never again could it be made whole, however skilfully the pieces were stuck together.

* * *

Kat paced, face flushed, eyes half-closed. Dragged from her sleep, without her jewels and fine clothes, she looked old.

"What have you done, child?" she asked, again and again. She wrinkled her nose in disgust. "And where have you been?" She held up her candle, for the curtains were still drawn in my bedchamber. She studied the soreness on my chin and around my lips, the mud on the hem of my cloak, my torn girdle. "Have you been with Dudley?"

"No. It's Tom Seymour who's betrayed me, Kat. He kissed me and—"

"A May Eve kiss is nothing," she said, too lightly. I had seen her face turn pale. "May Eve makes fools of us all, bewitches us all as much as midsummer with its new scents that make a woman swoon. But you surprise me, Bess. Surely you learned that lesson from your mother."

I glared at her. "My mother didn't live long enough to teach me," she said. "*You're* to blame for this, Kat. You should have protected me, but you simpered and giggled

and blushed every time Seymour came into sight."

"*I* did not kiss him."

"Neither did I." I wept piteously. "He kissed me. He saw that I was distracted and took advantage of me. Don't you understand, Kat? It's twelve years to the day since they took my mother to the Tower and now Tom's tainted me. I've tried so hard to lead a good life, but he's snared me."

"Listen, Elizabeth, you're *not* to blame. *He* is in the wrong, sniffing around the King's sister. Your mistake was going out alone at night."

I did not allow Kat to wash me before I went to bed. I lay in the filth of Bedlam that dawn. It was my penance for hurting Lady Catherine. As I tried to sleep, I thanked God that I had not babbled about Bedlam. Would Robert search for me there if I did not appear at the May Day joust? There would be no joust for me. I was tainted by scandal.

I never forgave Thomas for one thing: he saw me as my mother's daughter. By kissing me, he must have believed that I was like her, and thus he believed her to be guilty.

Sleep would not come. When I went into Kat's chamber to be comforted, I found her kneeling in prayer – and crying. Then I knew that the threat was great. I knew that the sword that had taken off my mother's head was hanging over mine.

Chapter Fifteen

In seventeen days, my mother was arrested, tried and beheaded. And seventeen days I waited for my punishment. No sugar roses. No egg whites for my skin. Nobody, except my own wretched self – and Kat. I hoped that Robert Dudley would ask to see me; but in my heart I knew that his parents would not permit it.

Lady Catherine announced that I missed the quiet of Hatfield Palace and would return there. I would not go to Gloucestershire for her baby's birth.

"Be thankful," Kat told me. "It's only Lady Catherine's love for you that might yet save your reputation. She understands what gossip did to your mother and she will protect you as best she can. As for Thomas Seymour, let's pray that he doesn't boast when he's drunk too much."

The roses were in full bloom the day I left Chelsea Palace – the roses that had led me to the river; the river that had led me to Francis. No fond farewells for me. Only a kiss from Jane, my little cousin, bruised and battered when she came here, now so much cleverer than me. Half-laughing, half-crying, and not understanding why I was leaving, she said, "Never to marry?"

"Never to marry," I whispered back. "Just two wise virgins."

When the litter was brought to the front steps – I was too weak and unhappy to ride like Kat – my stepmother showed herself. I threw myself at her feet and wept. It would have been better if I had not, for she took them for tears of remorse. At last, she took pity on me and spoke, fixing me steadily with her grey eyes. "I shall choose my words carefully, Elizabeth, for we both know and agree that once they are spoken, they cannot be returned. Your mother was vain and foolish, like my husband. I knew what he was when I married him, and why he married me, and I know that I love him more than he loves me. This could be his downfall, Elizabeth, and yours. The people will hate you if they hear of this because their hatred for your mother is never far from the surface. They will lick their lips at the scandal." I shuddered at the word. "You are young and Tom should not have abused you in that way. You have one of the finest minds I have ever met. In time, with wisdom and guidance, you will go far beyond the Tower that took your mother...as far as the throne of England if you take care. But I cannot be sure that you will be safe from this scandal."

I burst into fresh tears. "How shall I manage without you?" I asked.

"You have managed without a mother all these years," she replied. "How will you know the difference?" She let me kiss her. "You are not out of the woods yet, Elizabeth. This scandal will haunt you for years to come."

In Chelsea Woods, no men came from the trees, except Robert Dudley. I did not expect to see him. He had made no contact with me. Even my brother had not sent a word of goodbye.

Kat helped me from the litter and rode to a discreet distance to let us make our farewells under an oak tree, thick with new leaves.

Robert dismounted. In the same woods where I had been called the Boleyn bastard, we faced each other. My heart lifted at the sight of him, until I saw that his face was a mask of dislike and anger. "I didn't need to look for you in Bedlam," he said. "There was talk of little else at the May Day joust…of you and Tom Seymour."

"*He* kissed me, Robert. I didn't kiss him," I said. "You feared Francis, yet the danger came from my stepfather." I was trying not to cry. "Alys told me the truth and I was so happy when I came back…so happy that I said too much. If Tom's tongue loosens and lashes out, he might seek out Francis…"

"Why? I don't understand."

"Tom is desperate for power, you know that. He'll

say that he uncovered a plot to topple the King and my brother will thank him and…"

"But Tom doesn't know Francis's name or where he lives."

"He has spies everywhere. How long would it take him to flush out a boy who works on the river?"

"It won't happen," Robert said, his voice more soothing. "You imagine it will because you're upset now. In a few days…"

"*In a few days* —" I almost screamed. "Lady Catherine says this scandal will haunt me for a long time. Robert, will you promise, although you dislike me today and you don't know what to believe…will you promise that if Francis or his mother are ever in danger that you will warn them to leave England? Give them money to go, if you have to. Will you, Robert? For me?"

His expression softened. "Yes, because *I* should have protected you better. I shouldn't have let you go to Bedlam alone." He took a rose from his cloak pocket and handed it to me.

I breathed in its beautiful fragrance, felt my mother in the shadows around me. "I don't know when we'll meet again, Robert. I won't be allowed to have visitors at Hatfield Palace, not even you. It will be worse than before, because now I've lost Lady Catherine's trust, perhaps her love."

Kat signalled that it was time to be on our way, but I did not want to leave him. He helped me into the litter, began to draw the curtains.

"Remember what you said at Shrovetide, Bess, when you spoke from your heart in public? *Life is an illusion. We all see what we want to see, whether it is real or not.* Pretend *this* is an illusion. Pretend that Francis is safe in France with his mother. If you don't, then you'll be as lost as they are."

I cried. I choked on the tears that I shed for my mother, for Lady Catherine, for Alys, for Francis – for the whole world. Robert held me. He did not try to kiss me on the lips as Tom Seymour had done, but he kissed the nape of my neck. My spine tingled, and I forgot all other kisses, even my mother's.

"God speed you and protect you, sweet Bess."

I looked at his face which was so dear to me. In the passage of time, his childish cheeks would harden, as no

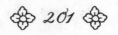

doubt would mine. His soft lips would tighten and I wanted to kiss them before they did. His skin would sprout black hair like Maggie Payne's, not soft gold as it was now, and I prayed that mine would not. "And you, sweet Robert."

At the last minute, he tried to kiss me, as he had done on my birthday, when I was his moon, his star, his fairy queen. I turned my face away. "No, Robert. We must love in private, *never* in public. We don't know who might be watching us. I'll have to live quietly at Hatfield for a long time, until the King invites me back to court. One day, Robert, when we're alone…"

"You'll always have me, Bess. Wherever you are… wherever I am."

We parted – he to return to London and me to take the dusty road to Hertfordshire.

I had come this way almost a year before with expectation of great happiness with Lady Catherine. Now I was returning to my palace in disgrace, alone, except for Kat and hanging over me a scandal that might haunt me for years to come.

I held Robert's rose all the way from London, peeling

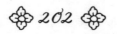

away the damp petals. By the time we stopped for our first night on the Great North Road, its petals had shrivelled in my hand.

Chapter Sixteen

Hatfield Palace, Hertfordshire

Scandal made a prisoner of me that lonely and cruel summer.

I had too much time to lick my wounds, to curse myself for what had happened. I went over the scene in the kitchen many times. *Had* I been to blame? *Had* I encouraged my stepfather in any way? I heard Lady Catherine's pitiful moan, saw her clutch her swollen belly as she called out, "Traitors!" and sometimes her face and belly became my mother's when she had let me pat her belly and promised me a baby brother.

When their faces haunted me to the point of madness, I sought fresh air. I walked in the garden where my mother and I had played hide-and-seek and lingered by the fountain where she had dangled me to cool my feet. And if it rained, I went to the nursery where she had steadied me on my rocking horse. I curled up on my little silver-tasselled bed, my mother's box and Lady Catherine's book side by side on the pillow, breathing in the scent of leather and roses.

As August gave way to early autumn days, I waited to hear the news of Lady Catherine's child. Would she forgive me in the joy of motherhood? Would she invite me to Gloucestershire to see her baby?

On my fifteenth birthday, a rider, dressed in Seymour livery, came early to the main door. I ran downstairs, only in my night robe, eager for news of her child, and for her invitation.

Kat was already at the open door, pale-faced, and by her side Blanche Parry was weeping. Kat held out her arms for me and I buried my face in her bodice. "My dearest Bess, Lady Catherine is dead," she whispered.

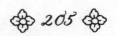

"Childbed fever took her as it did poor Jane Seymour. I said it would be dangerous at her age. Tom Seymour has a healthy daughter, named Mary."

I sank into grief at once. I was carried to my bed, almost senseless with the sorrow of it. By nightfall, my body was swollen with dropsy, worse than last Christmastide, more swollen than the bodies that Francis took from the Thames.

In the weeks that followed, Lady Catherine's death took me to the brink of madness. I had seen enough lost souls in Bedlam to make me fear losing my mind. I held onto it, although I stared into the abyss many times.

"Am I with child, Kat?" I asked.

"Foolish girl, of course not," she said. "One kiss doesn't make a baby – only a fool," she said.

When I came to my senses, every tree stood leafless, every flower long gone. The silver woods of Chelsea and the hell of Bedlam were as far away as the moon that was now sharp with frost.

❊ ❊ ❊

When I was well enough to be left with Blanche Parry, Kat visited London. Without her, the restlessness that comes from anxiety overwhelmed me. I fretted for Francis in his gruesome boat, and Alys, chained to her wall.

Kat came back bursting with news of Thomas Seymour – unwelcome news.

"Tom Seymour weeps for his dead wife and baby; but he keeps her ladies-in-waiting to serve you when you marry him."

"Tom Seymour boasts of becoming your brother's Protector with bribes of money and sweets. If he doesn't curb his behaviour, he'll be in the Tower by Christmastide."

"Tom Seymour talks of a secret plot to take the throne from your brother. If he can find out who the plotter is, he'll have the fellow hung, drawn and quartered and spiked on Traitor's Gate."

Tom. Tom. Tom. It hurt my head.

I had fretted. Now I feared for Francis. I even feared for myself.

Thomas Seymour is not a man to have his power

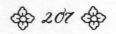

curtailed, I thought. If he cannot have the King in his grasp by marrying me, will he expose Francis, proclaiming himself a more worthy Protector than his brother Edward? *Another pup mewling for its master,* he had said on Twelfth Night. *Such pups should be drowned at birth.*

I had asked Robert Dudley to warn Francis of any danger. Had I asked too much of him? Why should he do it? How *could* he? I longed to be able to warn Francis. But Bedlam was too far and I was still too weak.

Two weeks before Christmastide, we removed briefly to Elsynge Palace in Enfield, less than a dozen miles from London. In our absence, Hatfield Palace would be cleansed and made ready for the twelve days of Christmastide, which we would spend alone, for no invitation had come from the King. It was no more than I expected, but I missed him. I missed everybody, even Mary.

Kat and Master Parry, my steward, had business in London. My isolation at Enfield hurt even more. So close to where I had lived so happily – yet now so far. In my still-tortured mind, I saw Lady Catherine, her pretty palace, her perfumed roses leading down to the river — all for ever beyond my reach.

Soon, it was other images that came to haunt me day and night. I saw Francis at the bottom of the Thames — because of me. I saw Alys still chained in Bedlam — because of me. They had given me back my mother and asked for nothing. Now I must give them something in return: a safe passage to France.

The months of near solitude at Hatfield Palace had taught me that there would be nobody to help me. I had once found the courage to go to Bedlam alone. Now I would summon up that courage to return.

It is easy to ride out on a foggy night. Everybody sleeps early, for there are no stars and no moon to keep them watching at the windows. Fog dulls and muffles every sight and sound. I would be no witch riding alone through the black night. I acted out the simplest illusion of all: I rode out as a man. I took my stallion, Troy, for he was swifter than my gentle mare. I led him slowly across the cobbles, slipping a coin into the gatekeeper's hands. Blanche Parry was sleeping like a baby when I left. Even if she had glanced at me in half-sleep, she would not have known me. I wore black breeches and black riding boots that had belonged to Edward, and they pinched my feet. I wore the black cloak that had hidden me last May Eve. It still stank of Bedlam.

My hair was troublesome. I twisted and pinned and netted it until my arms ached. I thought of the piglet boys from Shrovetide. I would wear no false beard, although I wished for more hair upon my chin, like Maggie's. My throat thickened at the memory of her kitchen, warm and sweet with sugar.

In my saddlebag were clothes for Alys, stolen from Kat. I could find nothing that would have fitted Francis. Inside my cloak pockets was enough money for their passage to France. I would force Alys to take it.

I was one of the unhappiest people to cling to a horse, so unhappy that Troy smelled my fear rising from me like the steam from his flanks. He reared and refused until I calmed him with sugar.

Mile after mile I galloped. On the Great North Road I feared walkers most. Riders and carters would have no need of a horse but an exhausted man on foot could steal Troy as soon as look at me. So I did not dare trot or canter.

As we plunged through the damp fog, I remembered the story that Maggie had told me, the one that every Gloucestershire child heard at its mother's knee – the one of a dying witch who regretted the evil she had done in her long life. She wanted a Christian funeral when she died, and she begged her children to tie up her coffin with chains so that the devil could not claim her back. They did as she asked. But the devil did come for her. He rode in on a horse with spikes ridging its back, to punish her for turning to God. He broke open the coffin chains, brought her back to life and sat her on his horse. "She can still be heard screaming in the hills," Maggie had said.

I was that wretched woman. Pains shot down my legs, through my buttocks, down my arms. Would I slowly die on the back of my horse and be condemned to ride this road for ever?

Grey fog, brown fog. Then the black fog that told me I was close to London. Before the city wall, I recognized Moor Field and its little church, its spire swallowed by

fog. In agony, I dismounted, tied Troy to a tree and entered the church. I sank to the flagstones, crying out in pain from my tormented limbs. The stink of the floor made me heave. Here people had recently relieved themselves, and not just of their sins.

Above me was Christ's body, bent low by his cross, the blood on his hands and feet seeping through the whitewashed walls. My father had destroyed the monasteries. My brother was destroying the churches. Such a waste, I thought, the whitewashing of the old faith into the new. One faith, one Christ. But I liked the new faith. Without it, I would not have been born.

I went the rest of the way on foot. It is a terrible thing to be alone in London after dark, even if you are dressed as a man. But soon I forgot my tormented limbs and strode like a man. No wonder men walk this world. They wear no dainty shoes and silk to slow them down.

This was no night of merriment and magic, of whispered secrets and softened footsteps like last May Eve. It was a night for evil, when the stench of the fog itself catches the back of your throat, and clogs it with terror.

When I had first come to Bedlam, I was haughty and arrogant, although I did not know it. I had thanked God that I had been born to the King and Queen of England. Now I saw the horrors with the eyes of an outcast myself and the sight unsettled me. The stone alcoves of London Wall were crammed with children who clung to my cloak, like leeches to wounds, sore-skinned, filthy-faced and barefoot. Their eyes begged. I wanted to give them money, but I dared not draw attention to myself, dared not risk being robbed of the money I carried for Alys.

If ever I were Queen, I would help these wretches. I would have them eating out of my hand and they would never go hungry again.

No questions were asked at the gate of Bedlam. The silver coin gave me entrance once more. I remembered to pay for a candle. Then I pulled my cloak around my face, held my breath and prepared to step into the filthy gloom.

Chapter Seventeen

Alys would weep again when she saw me. She would say that I was as brave as my mother. My agonized limbs hardly carried me through the vile cloisters where screams pierced my consciousness and set my heart racing, to the windowless corridor to her cell door.

I paused. There was no scent of rosemary and mint and may blossom – only a sour stench. I smiled at my foolishness. It was now December, not May and their scent would have long since died. There was no clicking of her knitting needles – only a scuttling and a scampering.

My heart thudded as I went in.

Alys's chains hung loose. Her ragged clothes were neatly folded next to them, wriggling with rats. I held my candle to every corner, to make sure that she was not huddled there.

Her cell was empty.

My heart lifted. Francis must have taken her to France.

I forced every aching muscle to move again. Like a drowning woman gasping for air, I ran through the cloisters. I would never have stopped running but for the creature that came from the shadows, whether at the sight of me or by chance I did not know. Wreathed in the fog seeping through the skylight, it rose, like a writhing sinner in hell's smoke; but only as far as its clanking chains would allow.

Hypnotized by the sound, I could not move. Then the creature tried to stand. It was a woman who must have once been tall and straight, now bowed by chains.

I held up my candle. "Alys?" I called. I saw that this

was some other woman, wrinkled and almost bald. She watched my candle shine onto a pool of water and bent down to lap it. My stomach heaved. I paused to let the feeling pass. Then I turned to go.

Behind me, I heard a sharp intake of breath, like a sword swishing through the air. The sound rooted me with fear. I shuddered, as if something cold touched my neck. It had happened, as I had always feared. A swordsman had crept up behind me and I was not kneeling in readiness; I had not made my peace with God or spoken my words of forgiveness. But there was no flash of silver, no pain, no eternal silence. Instead a voice called, "Traitor!" and rough hands gripped my neck through the bars, knocking off my cap.

I fought with the fury of somebody who fears that death is close. Pushing my feet against the bars, I pulled myself away long enough for the hands to briefly slacken and release me. I slumped to the ground, hair uncoiling, desperate for breath.

The angry voice quietened to a whispered question: "Lady Elizabeth?"

I looked up at a young man. His face and clothes

were blurred in front of me, but I made out his turquoise hose and the orange silk that showed on his velvet sleeves and breeches. He wore a short ruff, though unhooked and hanging loose, and an orange plume in his cap. Where had I seen these clothes before? As my breathing calmed, I saw that the buttons had been torn from his doublet, the buckles from his shoes.

They were Robert Dudley's clothes, though now the worse for wear. He had worn them when he came to dine on my birthday. But it was not Robert clutching the bars. It was Francis.

Since May Eve, he had grown more and more like my father as a young man – in the fullness of his lips, in his red-gold beard, now matted and stiff with dried spittle. He took off his cap, made a short bow. Only his hair was different. He had tugged out handfuls, exposing the sores of scrofula.

"Francis? What are you doing here?" I asked. "Where's your mother?"

His eyes wandered up to the rotting roof and back to the filthy flagstones. Then they settled on my face. He drew back his lips over his dirty teeth and laughed, so strangely that I did not know whether he might be mad or not. "I wanted nothing of your world," he said. "I told you that on May Eve. It's false, where a promise means nothing, where only lies flourish…"

"Where is she?" I asked again.

"She's dead."

My heart lurched. I must have cried out loud enough for the old woman to tell me to stop my woman's wailing. I touched Francis's cheek and watched his tears twinkling in the candlelight, each one as perfect as the pearls on Lady Catherine's brooch.

"*How?*" I asked. He did not reply and I rattled the bars to keep his attention. "I've not ridden like the devil all the way from Enfield only to ride back without knowing."

"Dudley came to warn me that your stepfather was wild with grief, wild for power, was asking about a red-haired boy in a death-boat," he replied. "He had to act before Seymour did, so he said."

"He's right. He promised that he would do it for me," I told him. "I've been ill, Francis, and alone…"

"…so I agreed to let him pay our passage to France.

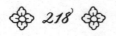 218

He sent in his clothes for me, and his mother's dress and a wig for my mother. She was beautiful again."

"When was this?"

"Ten…twelve days ago," he replied. "We had to wait for the right tide to take us to Gravesend. My mother boarded the barge quietly, made no fuss until we were in the middle of the Thames. Then she begged to be brought back here. When I refused, she threw herself into the river, just past London Bridge, where…"

I pictured Alys in the water, where the river churns against the bridge, her beautiful dress floating, her wig toppled by the current. I imagined Francis's skilled hands reaching for her, except that the sides of the barge would be too high.

"The guard said that when some people are given their freedom, they want to return to their prison. I refused to go to Gravesend alone…" Francis paused to sniff back his tears. "I had to find her body. I rowed up and down the river until…until she came back to the surface. I weighed her down with stones and let her drop…"

I could not let myself weep with him. If I did, I would never have stopped. I would never have had the strength to ride back to Enfield. "How did you end up *here*?" I whispered.

"The barge man must have sent word to Dudley. *He* brought me. Or rather, he paid some of those men outside to drag me."

Anger raged through me, so great that I struck the bars and the clatter brought other wretches from the shadows, rattling their chains as if to protect Francis from me. "I'll never forgive him," I shouted. "He had no right to do it…unless it was to protect you from Tom."

"He did it to protect *you*, not me. He knows that nobody believes the truth in Bedlam. We all know it." Suddenly, his face took on a different look – of fear and panic. "I can't stay here. My mother could ignore the hell that she was in. *I* can't."

As I listened to him, my mind was racing. How could I help Francis? If I paid to have him released now, where would he go? Where would he be safe? I could not be seen with him. My disguise would not fool for long.

"Francis, what shall I do?" I asked.

His eyes hardened at my question. "It's not for me to decide," he said.

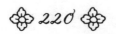

"*Please*, Francis. Tell me." He did not reply. If he had begged to leave Bedlam with me, I could not have refused. But he was not a man to beg, I knew that. I wiped the grime from his cheek with my glove and kissed his still soft skin. "I don't know what to do," I whispered.

He turned his back on me and was soon lost in the seeping fog.

I fled from Bedlam. Some of the children followed me to the little church and I paid them to lift me onto Troy. As I rode back to Elsynge Palace, the damp dawn did nothing to dry my tears. Near Enfield, the fog lifted. I remember being taken from my horse, washed, put to bed. Blanche asked no questions. Like Kat, she did not want to know the truth.

Chapter Eighteen

Hatfield Palace, Hertfordshire
21 January, 1549

Less than an hour ago, a scream tore me from my sleep and I ran outside, only to learn that Kat and Master Parry had been taken to the Tower.

Now Tyrwhitt is holding out the silver dish to me. Close-up, I see that the sugar roses it holds are misshapen, like baby cabbages, not made with Maggie's skilled fingers. Unlike Blanche Parry, Tyrwhitt is after the truth now as much as I ever was. He knows about the sugar rose that Thomas Seymour brought to my bedchamber in Chelsea Palace. If he knows that, how much more does he know?

Only time will tell. The thought of the days to come sickens me as much as the thought of eating one of the sugar roses.

"Sugar stirs the blood like nothing else, does it not?" he asks. "Try one."

"I am not a child to be tempted with sweet things," I say, stupefied.

He bites into one of the roses and I see that he is not accustomed to such sweetness, because he has lost none of his teeth, although the bottom ones lean like tombstones.

How *does* he know about the sugar rose that Tom Seymour brought to me on my birthday? It cannot be from Kat, unless he questioned her last night. Was it from Thomas Seymour himself, or his cook, Maggie Payne?

I want to run away from him as I did from Seymour, but I am too afraid. "Am I your prisoner?" I ask.

Tyrwhitt smiles briefly, his lips pale with sugar. "No, of course not."

"You have already arrested Kat and my steward, so if I rode from my palace now, would you call your guards to bring me back?" My voice drops to a whisper. I am thinking of my mother, taken from Greenwich Palace, in broad daylight for all to see her shame.

"Ah…well…yes. If you left before we had talked, I would think you guilty, madam. The King and his Protector thought that, in view of your youth, you should not be questioned in the Tower."

"So I *am* your prisoner, and therefore I must be on trial."

He glances around the schoolroom. "Do you see other men here who will judge you? No. We are alone, just to talk."

But he does not talk. He looks lovingly at my books on the table, as if he wants to teach me rather than interrogate me. Tyrwhitt picks up a volume of Virgil and flicks through the pages until he reads: "… *latet anguis in herba.*" He pronounces the Latin words as skilfully as I would. "There is a snake lurking in the grass," he translates.

"I know what it means, sir. I knew that when I was ten years old."

"*Who* is the snake lurking in the grass?"

Does he mean Francis or Tom Seymour?

My brave show of confidence deserts me. Terror uncoils in my belly and takes me by the throat. I cannot speak. Scarcely more than a month since my last ride to Bedlam and still the horror of it stretches my nerves to breaking. Blanche Parry never asked where I had been that foggy night, neither did she tell Kat that I had left the palace. Kat put my low spirits down to loneliness and the loss of Lady Catherine.

Tyrwhitt is waiting for my reply. My mind produces something witty, in spite of the trembling body that keeps it alive. "I know only one thing about snakes," I say. "A snake never stays the same. When it casts off its skin, it is a new snake. It can strike again and not be recognized."

"Mmm…yes, you are right." He puts the book carefully in its place. "So let us begin. From this last Christmastide to Twelfth Night, there has been talk of nothing else at court: Thomas Seymour – and you. He has sought to marry you since Lady Catherine's death last summer. He boasts to all who will listen – and that includes Mistress Ashley – that he kept on his wife's ladies-in-waiting to serve you. If he is accused of planning to marry you without the King's consent, he may face a charge of…treason." He curls his tongue over the last word. "If there is anything you wish to confess now, it would be seen – as I said – as youthful *folly*."

Ah – now we have it. He has spelled it out as clearly as Kat used to spell my first words. He wants evidence against Thomas Seymour. If I admit to youthful folly, he will use it against him. He will not care that my reputation is sullied.

But – and this is far more dangerous – if the King thinks that I agreed to marry Seymour without his permission, this is a treasonable offence for us both.

Once I would have laughed at the last charge, for it is too ridiculous to be true. But now I cannot laugh. Kat is in the Tower. Concern for her makes me moan, as Lady Catherine did on May Eve. I cannot bear to think of my dear Kat in that dreadful place, never knowing if…or when…they will come for her.

"Do not harm Kat," I plead. "*Please*. She has done nothing wrong."

He leans forward. "And – *you*?"

I lean too and we almost touch, for we both have large noses. I raise my voice so there can be no mistake. "I cannot answer for my stepfather, but *I* would never marry without the King's permission. I would do *nothing* that would cost me the throne of England."

"A young girl could be flattered by such a man as Lord Seymour."

"Flattered?" I give a little laugh, loud enough to show my disdain. "I am Henry the Eighth's daughter. *I* am the one with power. My stepfather is a man who desires it, like most men. To marry me would have been a triumph for him, not for me. That is why I would have refused him if he had asked. In fact, I shall never marry at all."

"Mmm…yes…so I have heard. And Lady Jane Grey too…"

Tyrwhitt's eyes alight on the sugar roses again, already melting in the heat of the fire. "Did Lord Seymour take sugar roses to Lady Jane Grey's bedchamber before she was dressed?"

"I do not know – I did not ask."

"Perhaps he favoured you above her? Why would that be?"

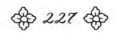

I am so filled with pride that I fail to see the snare he has set. I think only of Jane with her prim little mouth and hollow chest, who would never make a great Queen like me, and when I reply, it is with careless, boastful words. "She is a child, sir, and I am a woman."

"Ah…" The rose petal sticks to his tongue and I am sickened by what I have said. His mind is sword-sharp and threatens to stab me.

His eyes gloat. He has caught me up to my neck in mud, like a fish that is as good as dead. I have said too much. Now Tyrwhitt knows that I am proud of my womanhood. He will think that I used it to attract Thomas Seymour.

Like mother, like daughter. That's what he thinks, although he does not say it.

Within the hour, he has snared me. Have I learned *nothing*?

Chapter Nineteen

28 January, 1549

"You were smiling in your sleep," Tyrwhitt says. He must have run out of peppermint pastilles, for his breath is sour.

It is only seven days since he took charge of my palace and I am exhausted. He has questioned me every day.

I startle at his voice and open my eyes. How long has he been watching me as I slept at the schoolroom table? Worse, did I shout out secrets in my sleep?

The fire hardly flickers and the windowpanes sparkle

with evening frost. I must have slept for a long time. Small icicles glint on the inside frame. Like jewels, they flash their rainbow light across the floorboards and onto my throbbing forehead.

"I'm still tired." I yawn and stretch and to my shame, sweat seeps from under my arms. "I sleep badly without Kat."

"Perhaps your conscience keeps you awake?"

"No."

Tyrwhitt is exhausted too. He huddles in his glossy brown fur. He does not want to be in my draughty palace. He wants to be in the warmth and glamour of my brother's court. Did he think that he would be gone by now, clutching my confession of my "youthful folly" with my stepfather or – and this is far worse, being a treasonable offence – of my agreement to marry him without the King's consent? To succeed in wrenching a confession from me would be a big feather in his cap.

Is Tyrwhitt's skin thick enough to return to the King's Privy Council without it? It seems so translucent in the candlelight.

He stifles a yawn. "Did you seek to marry Thomas

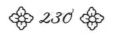

Seymour without the King's permission?" He must have asked me this question a thousand times. And I have answered a thousand times, "I would never marry without the permission of the King and his Privy Council."

"Did you behave foolishly with Thomas Seymour when you lived at Chelsea Palace last year, when your stepmother was still alive?"

I do not reply. I know when to be silent. This is not a treasonable offence, although it has sullied my reputation, and so I shall never admit it.

I curse my stepfather in my mind. It is because of him that I was sent away from Chelsea Palace and did not see Lady Catherine before she died, or the living daughter that she bore. Sorrow makes me flippant. It always does. "That is only two offences," I say. "My mother was accused of twenty-one."

"I can find more if you wish."

"She was accused of unseemly behaviour with her brother," I say. "Have you questioned *my* brother...the King?"

Why did I say it? I seem to have the devil in my mouth.

He is as horrified as I am. "Your vile words do you no justice, Your Grace. I advise moderation." Tyrwhitt taps the edge of the table. "Well, we have all the time in the world, unlike those in the Tower. Let us rest. I shall go to my bed and you to yours."

I drag myself to the garden door. My bones ache.

My eyes frighten me. In the window glass, they are as shrunken as an old woman's.

It is Tyrwhitt's habit to bait me when I have almost escaped. As I turn the handle, he says, "Whatever Mistress Ashley confesses, she has shown herself unfit to care for you, the King's sister, and she will not be allowed to return here, even if she is freed…or if you are still here." I swallow hard, but the lump in my throat almost chokes me. "I have asked my wife to be your new companion."

My voice trembles. "I don't want your wife. I want Kat. Send her back to me, sir." I am crying again. I am sick of my tears, for they do not cool me. They scald my cheeks. And they make me a child, not a woman. "She's all I have, sir. Don't take her from me."

Every tear must weaken me in Tyrwhitt's sight, for I cannot control them. Yet he is moved enough to pat my

hand and summon Blanche Parry to take me to my
bedchamber. By dawn, my hands and feet are swollen
with dropsy.

Chapter Twenty

5 February, 1549

Tyrwhitt reeks.

The smell is on his skin, his hair, his beard – the smell of my brother's court, of music and dancing, of all the things that I miss. Although I dislike it, my feet dance.

The door – the one that leads to the Great Hall – bursts open to reveal his wife, this tall Elizabeth, elegant in her high-necked dress of dark silk, who barely curtsies in the doorway. It is her perfume I smell on his skin. He must have sent for her, although I do not want her.

Her disdainful glance reminds me that I have neglected my appearance. I look down. Yes, the bodice of my dress is stained. My fingers are so swollen that I cannot wear my rings.

Tyrwhitt clears his throat. "Elizabeth…my wife, Elizabeth," he says. "She has come to stay."

So it is done. Kat will not come back to me now and I must bear it as best I can, although it is like torture to me. I can hardly stand.

"*Princess* Elizabeth," I respond. I force myself upright, and smile so as to appear a young girl, although I feel like an old woman. "Welcome to my palace, madam, although I did not invite you. No doubt you are impatient to see your husband, since I have detained him far too long, as he has detained me, a prisoner in my own palace."

"I have prayed for you, Your Grace." She towers above me, although I stand as tall as I can.

"Why?"

Her small eyes travel up and down my swollen body. "And so has Archbishop Cranmer. He sends you a gift to bring you solace." She hands me the most beautiful

book I have ever seen. Cherubs and angels crowd its dark red cover, around golden letters: *The Book of Common Prayer*. Cranmer is my godfather and this is his great work of translation from the Latin version.

"I do not want it," I say. "He has not been a loyal godfather to me." I throw it onto the table. "What news from London, madam? Births, marriages…" I stop myself.

"The Act of Uniformity has been passed. By spring, everybody will have to worship from Cranmer's prayer book."

"Not *that* sort of news, madam. I mean news from the Tower. Have you seen Mistress Ashley?"

"Yes, Your Grace. She has been moved to a more suitable room…" My heart leaps with relief. "… a more suitable room for questioning. It is the darkest room in the Tower, so dark that it is impossible to distinguish night from day. Unfortunately, there is no glass in the window. She says that she is too cold to sleep."

I bite my lip. "Please let her have a fire. She hates the cold. *Please*."

"Perhaps she will, one day." Tyrwhitt smirks. "We

have not had a burning at the stake for many years."

My breath quickens. Kat has too much air in her draughty prison. I do not have enough in mine. "Open the window, *please*," I beg.

"No!" Lady Tyrwhitt says. "An east wind is blowing today."

Devil's breath, Kat called it.

The stench of Lady Tyrwhitt's perfume sickens me. When she escorts me back to my bedchamber, I forbid her entry. "If you are to live in my palace, madam, leave off your perfume. You smell like a cat on heat and it makes my stomach heave."

She recoils. I thought she might slap me as you do a wilful child. But she only whispers furiously, "*You* were the cat on heat." Then her eyes brim and she looks away from me. "I was with Lady Catherine when she died. It would have broken your heart to see her."

I clench my teeth so tight that they tingle. I ache for my stepmother almost as much as my mother.

Taking advantage of my changed mood, she follows

me into my bedchamber. "What do you want, madam?"
I shift, uncomfortable.

"There is other news from London," she begins, "…of
a more delicate and private nature…and not for my
husband's ears."

"Ah – *London* news," I reply. "You mean gossip."

"I should tell you that this gossip has not died down,
madam. Rather, it has grown. I thought that it would
not settle, but melt away like first snow. But it has
hardened into ice." She pauses, pleased with her poetry,
and stares at my belly. "They say that you are carrying
Lord Seymour's child."

Anger, astonishment, panic – all quicken my heartbeat
and bring my voice to a breathless whisper. "Do I look
as if I am with child? I have not seen my stepfather since
last May Eve."

"They say that you visited him in London, in the
autumn…when he boasted of marrying you."

The devil grips my chest again. "I did not visit him.
How could I? I have been unwell ever since I left
Chelsea Palace."

"Mmm…when you left Chelsea so suddenly…that

illness is the cause of the other gossip," she continues. "It is as vile and as foul as the first, but you should know what it is…"

I push her through the door. "All gossip is foul, madam, and I have had enough to last me a lifetime."

I take to my bed. I often do and it serves me well. But I reckon without Lady Tyrwhitt. Kat used to bring feverfew and rosemary and lavender posset. Prayer is Lady Tyrwhitt's remedy. She prays, morning, noon and night. She is everywhere, even outside my privy.

The water seeps at last from my body. I am slender once more. "As you see, madam, there is no child," I say.

She cannot let it go. She leans towards me, whispering, "There is still the *other* gossip. I tried to tell you. A midwife has come forward to tell us that last autumn, around the time of your fifteenth birthday, she was summoned to the house of a nobleman somewhere in Hertfordshire, where a young woman of about your age, with long red-gold hair, gave birth to a healthy male child, which was taken from her." She pauses so that I can take this in, because she has seen the look of incomprehension on my face. "It is said that you gave birth to Lord Seymour's son. There is a great scandal hanging over you, madam."

She throws out her arms to me. She wants me to run to them and weep for the loss of my phantom son.

This is how it must have been for my mother when slander was heaped upon her head. Did she laugh in her strange way, or did she protest, as I do now?

"Lies," I shout. I do not care who hears me. "All lies. I am as pure as the Virgin Mary. Or does London gossip think that I was chosen like her for a virgin birth?" I point my finger at her. "This has come from *you*, madam. Only a woman knows how such spiteful talk dishonours."

"No, no, My Lady, it wasn't me. Who knows where such gossip begins?"

"But we know where it ends, don't we? It spills into the Thames and takes its victims to the Tower." I am almost crying. "I shall write to my brother, demand that he denies this slander in public. If necessary, I shall ask to be examined by his physicians who will—"

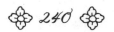

She blushes. "How do you know of such things?" she asks.

"Needs must when the devil rides," I reply. "This is how it was for my mother, accused of such scandal that she was glad to lose her head." I can hardly control my rage. "Do you think that I would lie with the husband of the only woman who has ever been a true mother to me?"

"Did your mother not lie with her brother so that she could bear a son?" she asks.

The inkwell is within reach. It is in my hands before I know it and I throw its contents over Lady Tyrwhitt. Black ink spots her cheeks and neck, like moles. Some settles in the puckers of her lips, puckered from too much praying, from too much gossiping. She scuttles away. "Send up more ink," I shout after her. "I must write to my brother *today*." My voice echoes into the stairwell. "If I do not write, *who* will?"

"It will not be worth the ink," she calls back. "There is already a confession from the Tower."

My heart almost stops. "Whose confession?"

She shrugs. "You shall know tomorrow."

When Blanche Parry comes to light the candles, she finds me kneeling. I have knelt so long that she has to lift me to my chair, as they did my father before he died. She rocks me as she used to rock my cradle, and I let her. She is all I have now.

At dusk, Lady Tyrwhitt remembers that she is here to soften me. She comes back. A deep ink spot still stains her left cheek, which she has tried to hide with white powder, and there is a fainter mark on her neck, half-hidden by her sapphire necklace. "We must not fight, Elizabeth, for we are stepsisters. Lady Catherine was also my stepmother. You know that she was married twice before she married your father?"

"So?"

"We should be friends if we are kin."

I shudder. "I already have one half-sister," I say, "and I have no need of another."

Mary, Mary, quite contrary, the daughter of my father's first wife, Catherine of Aragon, with Spanish eyes as dark as mine so that we cannot read each other's thoughts, who hates my mother so much that the hatred spoils her once pretty face. Mary, who used to live with me here when I was young, always weeping with migraines and woman's pains.

It is more than a year since I saw her at Twelfth Night, frowning at me as she touched her crucifix as if to protect herself from the devil.

I dismiss Lady Tyrwhitt. Tomorrow, I face the devil – her husband. And he will hold my life in his jewelled hands.

Chapter Twenty-one

6 February, 1549

I did not sleep last night. A brutal wind blew the riders in from London – I noticed hoof prints in the snowy courtyard this morning. Every tree is touched with frost. The fountain where my mother cooled me shimmers with ice.

A confession – whether it is Kat's or Tom Seymour's – could decide whether I live or die.

This is how it must have been for my mother. I am glad that she had Alys to comfort her before she died.

❉ ❉ ❉

Blanche Parry, my old nurse, does not know how to console me. "I've done nothing wrong. Neither has Kat," I cry. "What if her poor body's been broken on the rack? What if they've pulled out her fingernails? What if Thomas Seymour's said—"

"Hush, I won't let them hurt you," she murmurs. Her melodious voice soothes me for a while. Then Seymour's face flashes in front of me. He is not a man to sit in the Tower staring at death. I feel his beard brush against my neck. My voice rises to a scream. "My stepfather will say that I bewitched him as my mother did my father. And they'll believe him. Like mother, like daughter."

Lady Tyrwhitt comes to fetch me early. We walk to the schoolroom in silence, taking the inside steps from the Great Hall, for she dislikes the snow on the garden steps. My tears are down to a trickle now, so light they could be taken for the gleam of sweat.

When I have entered the schoolroom, Lady Tyrwhitt locks the door on the outside. I run to the garden door. It is locked too. Tyrwhitt is standing in front of a good fire, sleek and fragrant, eyes shining. The flames in the

hearth leap so high that they threaten to light the chimney. The room is stifling.

He glances down.

On the table, held open by the books of great men – Virgil, Horace and Cicero – is a parchment so fresh I can smell the ink. Whose confession is it? Seymour's? He could take me to the Tower if he wanted his revenge because I refused him. Is it Master Parry's? *He* has nothing to confess. But I know that in the Tower, you can confess to anything. People tell lies, *in extremis*.

Let it be Kat's. What she does not know, she cannot tell. *Can* she? But what if her body lies broken on her straw mattress?

The devil grips my chest. "I must have air, Sir Tyrwhitt." I am gasping like a drowning woman. "You know I hate to be shut in."

"There is air enough here."

But he brings me my chair and helps me to sit and gives me time to compose myself. "Who has confessed?" I ask.

"Your precious Kat."

Relief calms me for a moment. I am safe from

Seymour. But it is not over. "Has she been harmed?" I ask.

"No. She would have confessed nothing but for your steward, Parry. He broke first. You did not know it, but he and Mistress Ashley supped too much wine at Twelfth Night and she told him about you and Seymour. When he confessed, she had no reason to hold back." Tyrwhitt leans over the parchment and clears his throat.

Here, in this room, Kat read heroic tales to me. Here Kat taught me to read them for myself. Here now I must listen to a story of foolishness and humiliation and pray that it does not contain anything that might incriminate me. I thank God again that I never told her about Francis or Alys. I also recognize the warning signs of my body: it shudders and my breath is shallow.

Tyrwhitt reads: *"Written on the third day of February, in the year of Our Lord, fifteen hundred and forty-nine, the confession of Mistress Katherine Ashley, companion to the Princess Elizabeth, as follows: that last year at Shrovetide, the Princess Elizabeth went out on a barge upon the Thames alone with the Lord Admiral Thomas Seymour, and at other times he came to her bedchamber and tickled her…and I am not worthy to govern the King's sister…"* He pauses.

I must stay silent. I must bear this humiliation.

"…The Lady Elizabeth once told me that the Lord Admiral loved her too well and that Lady Catherine came suddenly upon them when they were alone and in each other's arms and fell out with both the Lord Admiral and her stepdaughter. This was why the Princess Elizabeth was sent back to Hatfield Palace…"

Tyrwhitt puts down the parchment. He plucks a quill from its pot and places it in front of me, with a fresh piece of parchment. "You may write your own confession now if you wish," he says.

He thinks that he has me, like Thomas Seymour did when he kissed me. He thinks that humiliation will loosen my tongue as it did before and take away my power. He thinks that because I have been foolish, I shall babble myself into confessing something I did not do. And he wants to use me to bring Seymour to the block.

I refuse the quill. I search every scribbled word of Kat's confession. "There is more," I say. "Did you think that I would not read it myself? *The Princess Elizabeth*

 *248*

when a man has a trick up his sleeve; Thomas Seymour taught me on May Eve.

My shoulders sag.

No, I am not out of the woods yet.

Chapter Twenty-two

14 February, 1549

I shall always remember that night when I danced under silver leaves, when I wore my leafy crown – when I was innocent. But I shall always remember the shame that followed, for it has made me a prisoner here. Now I am once again in the darkest part of the wood, where a man threatened me, where danger still lurks.

Somebody searched my chamber yesterday. A forbidden perfume lingered on my pillows and on my sheets, the one that makes my eyes water.

Elizabeth Tyrwhitt's perfume.

Does she think I have no sense of smell?

She must have come in when I was walking in the garden. Tyrwhitt has lulled me. He has left me alone this last week, ever since the confession came – until yesterday. His wife disturbed the books on my writing desk. She rearranged my gloves. Was she searching for my mother's box? If not – what else? What does Tyrwhitt know? Does he want the perfume box to accuse me of witchcraft? Does he know that Francis gave it to me? Does he know who Francis is? If I give him what he wants – what I *think* he wants – do I risk opening Pandora's box? The threat from Tyrwhitt is as great as the threat from Thomas Seymour, except that Tyrwhitt is far cleverer. He does not give up his prey so easily.

And I have nobody to protect me.

Today is Shrovetide. There will be no feasting or dancing on ice or illusion for us. Tomorrow, forty days of fasting for Lent.

And I must be done with Tyrwhitt. If I cannot outwit him today, I shall lose my wits. I must use them before I become ill with fear.

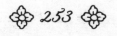 *253*

My head creaks and groans like an ice-bound ship, waiting for the wooden planks to split under the crushing ice.

If I do not outwit Tyrwhitt, there will never be a crown on my head, for I shall have no head to wear it. If I am to survive, I must change my skin as a snake does.

I am the daughter of the King and Queen of England. And Sir Robert Tyrwhitt will know it when he sees me. It is time for silver and silk and the soft sheen of pearls.

He *will* have his illusion today.

When I call for Blanche Parry, she comes at once. She opens the oak chest at the foot of the bed, shakes out my white and silver dress, the glorious dress that I wore for my last portrait, just before my father died. It is richly embroidered with flowers, a pearl at each centre. Its wide sleeves have silver cuffs. It still fits, for I have grown thin these last months. Only the bodice is tight over my breasts. And the sleeves are too short, but I do not mind, for they reveal my elegant hands. Pearls to brighten my skin — the three-pearl pendant made to match Lady Catherine's – and pearls at my ears and fingers, *and* circling my waist on a thin girdle.

"Leave my hair loose," I tell Blanche. "I like it that way. I shall curl it around my finger to remind Tyrwhitt that I am a Tudor, to remind him that one day a crown might sit there."

Blanche weeps with pride, remembering my past splendour.

It is noon. I have kept Lady Tyrwhitt waiting, pleading pains in my head and stomach. Kat used to bring me feverfew, but Lady Tyrwhitt prayed for me. She still suspects that I am with child, even though the swelling of dropsy is slight.

When I have sent Blanche for Lady Tyrwhitt, I take the perfume box from its hiding place. I kiss the falcon crest. It is my last link to my mother and I might have to do without it.

Lady Tyrwhitt sinks into a deep curtsy when she sees me. She did not mean to do it. I can see it by the surprise in her eyes. She acted from instinct.

❖ ❖ ❖

Tyrwhitt is asleep, sitting up. His eyelids twitch. When he hears us enter, he struggles to stand and groans at his aching knees.

But it is into his eyes that I look, for I need to understand him. I see what I need to see: the look of a man who has sought greatness all his life and craves to be in the presence of it.

He sinks into a bow until I command him to sit. I stand as I stood for my portrait. He must have seen it many times, for it has hung at Whitehall Palace these past two years: eyes looking straight at him, mouth firm, hands – my beautiful hands – holding a book. I have forgotten the book.

"Leave us," I say to his wife, "and give me back the key to my schoolroom."

She is astonished at the queenly command in my voice. She glances at her husband, arching her eyebrows in a question and he nods. She places the key on the table and I put it in my pocket.

Tyrwhitt watches, body tense. From my dress, he knows that this is the last game between us. One of us will win today.

With a flick of my wrist, I conjure the perfume box from my sleeve, as Francis did. How it gleams in my hand. Yes, silver is my colour. "If you wanted it so much, sir, why did you not ask for it?" I say.

He is clever. He gives a short laugh, feigns surprise. "Ah, yes, the *box*. The maids say that it contains a love potion that you used to enchant Thomas Seymour, that you smeared it on your body and on your lips at night. They say that when you used it, your face became lovesick. Or did you use it to hide the stench of sin?"

I laugh in return, although it is the laugh that Kat dislikes – my mother's laugh, halfway between despair and terror. At the look on his face – as if it has evoked a memory of her – I calm myself.

He peers at the crest and then backs away as if the falcon's claws will tear at his skin. "Did you accept it as a bribe?" he asks. But the words are hollow, as if he has said them in his head too many times.

"No." My voice is tight. "It was a gift from my mother," I say. "Have you forgotten that all her belongings were banned or burned or buried? This is all I have of her. It is the sort of gift a mother gives to a daughter, is it not – perfume?" I push up the lid and he recoils. "My mother was a sacrifice. The first perfumes came from the fragrant leaves thrown into the fire to hide the stench of burning sacrificial flesh…*per fuma*… from the smoke. She was sacrificed so that my father could marry again to have a son."

In the warmth of the fire, the lingering perfume scents the air as if she has entered the schoolroom: her hair brushes my face, her lips kiss mine, and she lifts my hair and nibbles the nape of my neck.

A beautiful rose, cut too soon, but still here to protect me. When this trial is over, when Tyrwhitt has left me in peace, I shall bloom in her place.

"It is no magic potion, sir, unless you want to believe it."

Tyrwhitt's eyes droop. He remembers my mother too for he knew her well when he was my father's servant. The potion has worked its magic, for his face softens. He forgets where he is, as I do. He is back in my father's court when my parents dazzled and were enchanted with each other, when he wanted a son so much that disenchantment came. "There are so many people who are afraid to remember her," he whispers. "Yet who could forget her?"

He does not take the box.

In the corner of the window, an icicle is melting. Its water trickles down the pane. Tyrwhitt gets up and wipes the glass with his cuff. A ray of cruel sun shows how exhausted he is.

If he does not want the box, what does he want?

Has he finished his dirty work here? Will he order his servants to pack? Will he order his horses to be made ready for the long journey to London? Will he and his wife disappear into the chilling darkness?

I slump into a chair with exhaustion. The sword has lain close to my neck these past weeks.

Tyrwhitt opens the window and he lets in the scents of early spring: crocuses and primroses and violets. He says, "Elizabeth," and I do not reply, thinking that he is calling for his wife. Chill air creeps into the stifling schoolroom and I lift my hair so that it can cool my neck.

Why is he still here? What does he want from me? Have I crowed too soon? I shall not turn round. I shall not speak.

He must have walked on tiptoe or taken off his shoes, for I do not hear him until his sour breath is whistling in my ear: "Elizabeth, have you ever been to Bedlam?"

This is the question that could seal my fate. I cannot breathe. I feel as if Thomas Seymour's lips are still suffocating me.

How do I answer it?

I shift in my chair. Pain darts through my body.

This February day is sinking early into night. Snow dusts the garden, lights the fountain.

I must gather the last of my wits. It is the play-acting that has distracted me these last weeks. Creating the illusion is the challenge and I have enjoyed the effect on my one-man audience, as illusionists and magic men must do. But I have forgotten my lines.

Tyrwhitt waits.

Maggie Payne told Thomas Seymour that I had gone out alone last May Eve. He – or Maggie – would not hesitate to tell Tyrwhitt, if asked – or tortured to tell.

I struggle to remember my lines. I stand and move to the window for air.

 260

"Your friend Robert Dudley has been seen lurking outside Bedlam's gates," he says.

It is the prompt that I need. "Why shouldn't he? You can pay to enter Bedlam for entertainment. They say that it's better value than the playhouse." A deep shudder of distaste runs through his body. "Not everybody in Bedlam is mad, sir. Women are often taken there by husbands who want to keep them silent, by fathers because their daughters will not marry the men they have chosen. It is a place for badly-behaved women."

He smiles. The colour comes back to his cheeks. "Have *you* ever been there?"

I give him something to keep him quiet. "Yes. Last May Eve."

Tyrwhitt blinks rapidly. Then he laughs. "I do not believe you. Mistress Ashley has never spoken of it. And the river was full of barges that night. Nobody has come forward."

I was right. He does not know. "Surely you remember that it was my mother's custom to visit the lost souls of Bedlam? Her brother was Governor of that hell on earth. Since she was taken to the Tower on May Day, it is the time I always think of her… Sometimes I go then, to visit in her name, to take may blossom. It fell onto her hair as she walked to the scaffold. Yes…I took may blossom to scatter on the floor, for you cannot imagine the stench of the place…sir."

He gulps. "Did you come back with your head full of fanciful thoughts?"

My heart quickens. What does he know? Was Maggie lurking in the shadows of the pastry room, her face flushed from her own a-Maying, or with jealousy because my stepfather was kissing me?

"There are no fanciful thoughts in Bedlam – only misery and degradation," I say. "I came home thinking of my mother."

"Yet less than three weeks later, you left Chelsea Palace under a black cloud."

"No, the sun shone all the way here." I smile. "I was tired of Chelsea Palace. Summer stinks there." I turn away from him.

"But why did you not go to Gloucestershire with Lady Catherine for the birth of her child, as Lady Jane did."

"I was exhausted. I needed the quiet of this palace."

He is behind me again, at the window. All these weeks, I have waited for the sword to fall and now I hear its swish through the air towards my quivering neck and I prepare myself for the blow.

Is it eight weeks since I went back to Bedlam? The horror of it still claws at my heart. The wounds are as fresh as if I were there. Francis was right. It will haunt me for the rest of my life.

Has Tyrwhitt seen what I saw there? Is it etched in his memory, as it is in mine? Does he hope that the horror of it will make me babble?

I see his chain catch the candlelight, reflected in the window, for it has long been dusk and the servant has not yet come to close the curtains. A few snowflakes flurry from the sleet against the windowpanes and some stick like flakes of wood ash. I watch them settle, see my pinched face staring back at me.

Is this how you look when you have been to hell so many times that you cannot find your way back? Is this what Virgil meant?

Has Tyrwhitt seen the secret Bedlam holds? He can still trap me into treason if he has.

Tyrwhitt clears his throat. It has become an irritating habit. "There is a boy…" he begins "…a stranger, who has the look of your father, God rest his soul…who rows up and down the Thames…"

My voice trembles with uncertainty. "London is full of such boys," I say.

"…plucking corpses from the river to earn his living."

"Somebody has to do it, sir."

"He has disappeared. He might be a danger to the King's person. He might be here to plot or cause harm… Seymour has asked about him." He drums on the window. Like me, he has worn a mask for many weeks. Unlike me, he lets his slowly slip to reveal a face that is consumed by anger, and frustration that a young girl can outwit him. "Your stepfather has let you down. He has let his King and country down. Now you have the chance to save yourself, to speak out against him."

"And if I do, you might turn the evidence against me," I reply.

Ask me about Francis! Ask me, I want to shout. Let the sword fall. *Now*.

Gripping the edge of the table, he spits out his question with the fury of wind and rain gusting together. "Do you know this boy?"

The cold blade lies across my neck. He thinks that he has me, for he sees my neck quiver. He thinks he will have a confession after all. Not to kissing Tom Seymour or agreeing to marry him; but for plotting against the King. Or some other charge that I do not know about, that I must deny as my mother did.

Can Tyrwhitt still outwit me? Has he already taken Francis to the Tower, to tug out the truth with his fingernails?

I rest my cheek against the cold glass of the window. Only my stiff bodice holds me upright. Tyrwhitt is next to me. But he dare not touch me. I am a princess. Instead, he places his face as close as he can, his nose almost touching mine. Close up, his beard reeks of stale food, although his breath is still sweet. Hair sprouts from his nostrils. His lips contort with anger, and there is a boil beneath his nose – if he shouts any louder, it will explode its pus into my face.

Tyrwhitt raises his hand, as if to prod me into replying.

He could still subdue me. He only has to take me to the Tower and I would break if I saw the place where my mother died.

He lowers his hand and prods me with his voice instead. "*Do* you know him?" Tyrwhitt is pressing his hands together because they itch to shake me, I am sure of it. He stands before me, legs planted apart like my father's when he grew fat. "God's Blood, give me patience!" he says. "Yes or no?"

Answer *yes* and I shall be pulled into a plot that I have not plotted. Like mother, like daughter. Answer *no* and I condemn my brother to remain in Bedlam. Answer *no* and I shall be safe. Who will believe what a man in Bedlam says?

Life is an illusion. If I don't believe that, I'll be lost.

I know one thing – I do not want to stretch out my pretty neck for the sword as my mother did. I want to be the Queen of England.

I cannot speak. My lips are too cold. I imagine Robert's kisses warming them and my voice comes from far-off, as if I am still wreathed in the fog of Bedlam. "No."

"You're lying."

"I never lie, sir."

"Your mother lied," Tyrwhitt says.

"Why would she lie to God?"

"Her friend Smeaton did," Tyrwhitt sneers.

"His mind was broken."

"Perhaps yours is broken, madam. Perhaps *you* should be in Bedlam?" His face takes on a look of piety. "Think, madam, of your conscience. How will you answer to God on the Day of Judgement?"

"I put my trust in man, not in God," I say.

"Then I ask you for the last time. Yes or no?"

Bedlam…a boy. They are like words whispered in the wind. One gust and they're gone. Tyrwhitt knows nothing more. If he did, he would not ask.

My breath comes in little gusts…Francis, my brother, who has nobody to protect him, or care for him now. I want to bathe his sores with camomile. But I must not. I have drunk the poisoned water of hell and my heart turns to stone.

My temples throb with the din of rattling chains. But Bedlam must be endured if I am to survive, even if it shackles me like a chain. In a gasp, I call out, "NO."

The melting icicle at the window cracks. Tyrwhitt has snapped it, as a neck snaps under the sword. He rests it against his flaming cheeks until it starts to melt and he throws it down. "On this occasion, I can find you guilty only of the folly of youth," he pronounces. "But if there is ever another occasion, you may not be so lucky..." He returns to the table and closes the lid of the box, before crossing to me and folding my fingers over it. His hands are as cold as death. "I do not want it, Your Grace. As you say, it is the sort of gift a mother gives to her daughter."

And he lets it be – as I must let it be.

He leaves by the garden door. He pauses as he always does, as if there might be more. "You have a fine mind, Your Grace," he says, bowing. "Use it well."

"I already have," I reply.

The door creaks. Then it slams behind him.

At last I am alone in my schoolroom. I stand at the window to watch him go and I see my mother darting in and out of the hedges playing hide-and-seek with me, dangling my bare feet in the water to calm me, her soft

lips against my cheek, her heavenly smile... Then I see Francis in Bedlam, waiting for me, and the shame of my betrayal weighs me down.

I cannot think about him now. I *shall* not think about him.

Tomorrow, I shall have roses planted all the way to the fountain and when I walk there – a strange occupation for a young girl whose feet long to dance – early in the morning and drink in their heavenly perfume, I shall hear my mother rustle in the early morning shadows and remember those who have protected me – Alys and Francis and Robert Dudley.

Tomorrow, I shall take off these fine clothes and put on sombre ones that speak of piety and innocence, until the mud that clings to me returns to the bottom of the river. And when it has settled, I shall wear the colours of the moon: white, cream and silver – and pearls to cool my Tudor hair.

I have always lived with lies. Now I must live with my own. I shall be careful whom I trust. I shall love in private. Not in public. I was born in the Chamber of Virgins and a wise virgin I shall remain.

And if…when…I am Queen, I shall bloom for my mother, a perfect rose cut too soon.

Exhausted, I sink to my knees. It is safe to do so. With Tyrwhitt gone, I fear no swordsman stealing up behind me to take off my head. Today, I shall not be condemned as my mother was.

I am safe – for now.

Author's Note

The interrogation of the young Elizabeth at Hatfield Palace during the winter of 1549 is well documented. The Thomas Seymour scandal was a dangerous rite of passage for the young Elizabeth, and brought comparison with her ill-fated mother, Anne Boleyn. Many historians believe that Elizabeth's decision never to marry was because of the horrific death of her mother.

I wanted to add another dimension to this scandal. What was it like for Elizabeth to grow up in the shadow of her mother – the first Queen of England ever to be executed? How far would Elizabeth go to prove her innocence, in her desire to remain unblemished so that she would be worthy of the throne of England? I decided to use the fictional characters of Francis and his mother – *and* the perfume box – to explore the development of Elizabeth's character more deeply.

All the other characters in this story are real.

I have exploited Elizabeth's documented character to the full. She *did* have a keen sense of smell like her father. She *did* hate bad odours and being closed in. She *did* love the sugar that rotted her teeth. She *did* love Robert Dudley, whom she nicknamed "Eyes". And she *did* suffer ill health through much of her adolescence because of the stress of the Thomas Seymour scandal.

The portraits described all exist, but may not have hung together as I suggest. I have taken a liberty with Elizabeth's portrait only. The dress in the portrait that I describe was made of pink damask. I chose white to remind readers that Queen Elizabeth always wore white and silver for her portraits to maintain her image as the Virgin Queen.

Within five years of this scandal – with the exception of Elizabeth, her servants, Mary, Robert Dudley and Mistress Ellen – all the other real people were dead: Thomas Seymour was executed for treason in March, 1549. His brother Edward was executed for treason in 1551. Lady Jane Grey, her husband Guildford Dudley, and his father John Dudley, were executed for treason by Queen Mary in 1554. Archbishop Thomas Cranmer was burned at the stake by Queen Mary in 1556.

Elizabeth was safe until her sister Mary became Queen in 1554 and sent her – with Robert Dudley – to the Tower for a suspected Protestant plot. She narrowly escaped execution, becoming Queen of England upon Mary's death in 1558 at the age of twenty-five. Elizabeth ruled for forty-four years. She never married. Robert Dudley, Kat Ashley and Blanche Parry remained faithful servants until their natural deaths. Elizabeth never forgave Robert Tyrwhitt, and when she became Queen, she banished him from court for the rest of his life.

Pauline Francis

Acknowledgements

I want to thank my family for their constant interest and support – especially my husband – also Megan Larkin and Anne Finnis for their comments on the manuscript.

A special thanks to Sam Whisker, chef and patissière, who made me a sugar rose as I watched her – and let me glimpse the pleasures and pitfalls of a world I know nothing about.

Bibliography

Ackroyd, Peter, *London: The Biography*, Chatto &
Windus, 2000
Arnold, Catherine, *Bedlam*, Pocket Books, 2009
Borman, Tracy, *Elizabeth's Women*, Jonathan Cape,
2009
Falkus, C. (Ed.), *The Private Lives of the Tudor Monarchs*,
Folio Society, 1974
Fraser, Antonia, *The Six Wives of Henry VIII*, Mandarin,
1993

Picard, Liza, *Elizabeth's London*, Phoenix, 2004

Plowden, Alison, *Lady Jane Grey: Nine Days Queen*, Sutton, 2003

Plowden, Alison, *The Young Elizabeth*, Sutton Publishing, 1999

Porter, Linda, *Mary Tudor*, Piatkus, 2009

Mumby, F & Rait, R. *The Girlhood of Queen Elizabeth: A Narrative in Contemporary Letters*, Constable & Co., 1909

Richardson, Ruth, *Mistress Blanche*, Logaston Press, 2007

Ridley, Jasper, *The Tudor Age*, Robinson, 2002

Salgado, Gamini, *The Elizabethan Underworld*, Rowman & Littlefield, 1977

Sim, Alison, *Pleasures & Pastimes in Tudor England*, History Press, 2009

Sitwell, Edith, *Fanfare for Elizabeth*, Macmillan, 1962

Starkey, David, *Elizabeth*, Vintage, 2001

Weir, Alison, *Children of England: The Heirs of King Henry VIII*, Pimlico, 1997

Weir, Alison, *The Lady in the Tower: The Fall of Anne Boleyn*, Jonathan Cape, 2009

Pauline Francis has worked as a school librarian and a French teacher, and spent time in Africa translating books before becoming a writer herself. She has written educational stories, such as *Sam Stars at Shakespeare's Globe*, focusing on her favourite subject, the sixteenth century, and retold classics such as *Oliver Twist*. She has written for young people learning English as a foreign language. This is her third novel for Young Adults. Her first – *Raven Queen* – a tale of love and tragedy based on the life of Lady Jane Grey, is set several years after the events in *Traitor's Kiss*.

Pauline is married with two grown-up children, and lives in Hertfordshire.

To find out more about Pauline Francis, visit her website: paulinefrancis.co.uk

Usborne Quicklinks

For links to websites where you can read more about the life of the young Princess Elizabeth, learn about the Tudor court and find out about Elizabethan England, go to the Usborne Quicklinks Website at www.usborne-quicklinks.com and enter keywords "traitor's kiss".

Also by Pauline Francis

Raven Queen

*I have lived the life of a princess since the day I was born.
But it did not bring me what I wanted. I am still trapped.*

*My beloved Ned speaks of love, freedom, a future. To walk with
him in the forest, our raven soaring above us, is my
only joy. But my father plans that I shall be betrothed to the
King and I am afraid. Queens of England have a habit of
dying. I have no desire to take the throne, no wish to
find myself in the Tower of London.*

Wife, Queen – I fear it will bring me to my knees.

Raven Queen weaves a mesmerizing tale of love and
tragedy based on the life of Lady Jane Grey, all too
often remembered as just a line in a history book.

9780746078808

Praise for *Raven Queen*

"Written in timeless language with a hint of the poetic in the spare prose, the book underpins the love story with thoughtful imagery and symbolism...The book has an enduring theme of religious intolerance, makes the 16th-century vivid and ends with an unforgettable twist".   *The Sunday Times*

"Francis' alternating first-person narrative weaves a fascinating story."   *Bookseller's Choice, The Bookseller*

"A visceral, mesmerizing debut novel...relayed through a series of thrilling, climactic tableaux in haunting, lyrical style."
                    TES Magazine

"An utterly fabulous read...Philippa Gregory for a younger audience."   *Rachel Forward, Gardners Books*

"This stunning and lyrical tale will hold readers captive and haunt them long after the last page has been turned."
                    Becky Stradwick, Borders

A World Away

I am afraid.

These pale-skinned men have killed my mother and betrayed my people. Now they have brought me to a place they call England where they want to display me in front of their 'Virgin Queen'.

My name is Nadie, but some call me 'savage'. I find it hard to endure their taunts, stares and insults. I do not want to live in this grey, inhospitable land.

And yet there is one boy, Tom, whose blacksmith's dark skin matches my own. When he looks at me the fire of love burns in my heart. I feel I could find happiness with Tom – but can his love for me survive in my world, with my people?

A World Away is a bold and beguiling story of
love and separation, set against the tragedy of the
first settlers in the New World.

9780746081129

Praise for *A World Away*

"A dramatic and heart-rending love story."

Georgina Hanratty,
Tales on Moon Lane in Publishing News

"It's a captivating tale of love, tragedy, immense danger and separation of two people so different and yet with so much in common. The author's characterisation is superb; the plot is heart-wrenching."

Louise Weir, www.lovereading4kids.co.uk

"Pauline Francis is masterful at turning dusty history into something alive & relevant – this memorable love story set in Plymouth and the New World in the 1580's is astonishingly good and deserves to be read widely."

Claudia Mody, Waterstones

"Beautifully and elegantly written, this story confirms Pauline Francis as a fine historical novelist." *Carousel*

"I found this book an amazing and interesting read and I couldn't put it down." *Teen Titles*

*For more compelling tales of
love and courage
log on to
www.fiction.usborne.com*